Tales from the Ashes

By the Fire: An Anthology of Stories by Algonquin College's Professional Writing Students, Volume 2

Algonquin College's Professional Writing Program et al.

Published by Spine Online Press, 2024.

This is a work of fiction. Similarities to real people, places, or events are entirely coincidental.

TALES FROM THE ASHES

First edition. April 25, 2024.

ISBN: 979-8224649907

Written by Algonquin College's Professional Writing Program et al..

Table of Contents

This anthology was written, edited, illustrated, and formatted by students in the Professional Writing program at Algonquin College in Ottawa, Ontario (Class of 2024).

Authors

Ailsa Allan | Comet C. | Alex Cuvelier | Rey Del R. | Gregory Dickey | Jack Dingwall | Zoe Farmer | Dalainey Gervais | Chris Hodgins | H. Issaq | Joel | Garrett Johnson | C. Kaneway | Eirini Katsika | William Keizer | Sarah LaHaise | Amy Lawford | Owen McDonald | Angie Mosher | Gareth Myers | Becca Nicholson | Milo O'Connor | Kaela Pacheco | Emily-Ann Petawabano | Valerie Robert | Nicholas Saumur | Edwin M. W. Smith | R. Solitairo | Abigail Wallingford | Paige Welburn | Chase Wonnacott

Illustrators

Abigail Wallingford (front cover)

Editorial Board

Editors-in-Chief
Alex Cuvelier & Angie Mosher
Prose Editors
Jack Dingwall | William Keizer | Sarah LaHaise
Managing Editor
Becca Nicholson

Full Editorial Team

Ailsa Allan | Lucas Allen | Owen Banham | Amber G. M. Boileau | Comet C. | Isabella Cooke | Alex Cuvelier | Rey Del R. | Gregory Dickey | Jack Dingwall | Zoe Farmer | Dalainey Gervais | Breanne Gormley | Keegan Hall | Chris Hodgins | H. Issaq | Joel | Garrett Johnson | C.Kaneway | Eirini Katsika | William Keizer | Sarah LaHaise | Amy Lawford | Dayton MacNeil | Owen McDonald | Christopher Mesidor | Angie Mosher | Gareth Myers | Wesley Naylor | Becca Nicholson | Milo O'Connor | Kaela Pacheco | Emily-Ann Petawabano | Chloé Potvin | Valerie Robert | Nicholas Saumur | Luca Schiavone | Edwin M. W. Smith | R. Solitairo | Andrew Stone | Kayleigh Vantour | Abigail Wallingford | Paige Welburn | Chase Wonnacott

Production Team

Gregory Dickey | Angie Mosher | Becca Nicholson | Edwin Smith | Kayleigh Vantour | Abigail Wallingford

Faculty Support

Nicole Chatelain | Michele Hall | Natalie Morrill

Special thanks to the Algonquin College journalism program for publishing advanced copies of the following stories in the online edition of the Algonquin Times *student newspaper:*

"Letters from Home" by Alex Cuvelier (December 8, 2023)
"Rot" by Jack Dingwall (December 14, 2023)
"A Date with Destiny" by Chris Hodgins (December 18, 2023)
"The Pact" by Garrett Johnson (December 18, 2023)
"Cowboys and Angels" by Angie Mosher (December 19, 2023)

Introduction

In the second printed edition of the By the Fire Anthology, we bring you Tales from the Ashes. It takes you through the life cycle of a fire, from the first spark to the final ashes. This edition is a collection of 31 short stories from the Professional Writing students at Algonquin College.

It's been our honour and great pleasure as Co-Editors-in-Chief to oversee the Line and Structural editing teams. The collection of stories presented here make us proud to count ourselves among these talented authors. We've seen first-hand the hard work our fellow students have put into writing and editing these stories, and the dedication and care that shines through each piece. For many of our contributors, this is their first time having their work published. It takes a lot of courage and vulnerability to share your writing. The editing process requires a writer to surrender control and allow someone else to take up the reins, something not always easily done. However challenging that may be, we can comfortably say it was with the utmost care and compassion that we edited and constructed these stories for this edition. As you read these carefully crafted and curated stories, we hope you can appreciate the journey the authors have been on and wish to take you through as a reader.

Not so long ago, we both lived very different lives in Nova Scotia. The land was different, the people were different, and our days were very different indeed. But the one thing that was no different at all was our knowledge that we always wanted to be writers. Our hope for this collection of stories that embodies the hope and dreams, the secret passions and open efforts of all the writers within, is that it inspires more writers to follow that dream. To know that, as far-fetched as it might seem, it can be done. We've have had many twists and turns in our journeys, but now we know for sure it's always better late than never.

Your Editors-in-Chief,
    Alex Cuvelier and Angie Mosher

Spark

We are born helpless. As soon as we are fully conscious we discover loneliness.
— C.S. Lewis

Letters From Home

by Alex Cuvelier

To say that my accommodations were modest would be a generosity beyond compare. The water stains on the crumbling plaster walls replaced elegantly brush-stroked canvases, serving as the artwork adorning my new abode. The maddening drip of rainwater from the ceiling and the blustering of wind through the cracked and rotting windows had replaced the familiar din of the bustling city. It's not as though I was accustomed to living in the very lap of luxury, but my position did afford me a life of relative comfort. How strange that it would be this same position that resigned me to living in this hovel. This backwater hamlet, whose name would be of little consequence to anyone other than myself or a passing traveller, was where I would spend the next few months surveying plots for my company's records.

At first, it was my displeasure to be here, to be away from my ambitions and responsibilities back home, that I attributed my uneasiness to. It was the long days of unrewarding work and unpleasant surroundings that I blamed for the sleepless nights. Then, one night, as I sat at the small table in the front room of my dismal abode, penning letters back home by candlelight, my head was turned upward by the sounds of skittering in the attic. I shuddered to think what manner of filthy provincial vermin I might be sharing this space with. This continued throughout the coming nights, leaving me bleary-eyed and weary each morning. Gradually, though, as the loneliness set in, I began to think of it as something of a pet. Though its nature was unknown and unseen, whatever was in the attic was my only company through the long nights.

In truth, I had all but begged to not be chosen for the task. I was the sole caregiver to my ailing mother—a responsibility that required much of my time and attention, and one that my soon-to-be wife was not fond of. Even less so now as the task passed to her in my stead. Nevertheless, my protests fell on deaf ears. I was assured that this task was of the greatest importance for my future success at the company. I was told by my supervisor, a man for whom I had little respect and even less admiration, that I was "rather fortunate," as I would be sent by locomotive and would arrive at my destination in just a few days. I was told that I should "relish the opportunity," and that this was a journey that would have taken my predecessor weeks by carriage. It was made clear that I was in no position to refuse.

After a particularly long day of dealing with the unhelpful locals, I returned to my small apartment to find a letter from my fiancée saying that my mother had mysteriously passed, taken by a sudden onset of illness. I wept long into the night. My desire to return home grew to an unbearable weight. As I sat drafting tear-stained letters, both to my fiancée thanking her for being with my mother in her last moments when I could not, and to my employer requesting to return home in light of her death, I heard the nightly skittering grow louder. Loud as the footfalls of a child running overhead. Exhausted, I passed it off as an overtired mind and a broken heart. I sealed the letters shut for tomorrow's delivery and laid down for another restless night.

After a few more days of dreary work and wakeful nights, I received another letter, this one from my employer. I opened it eagerly. I had been awaiting their response allowing me to return home and attend to the matters of my mother's funeral arrangements. To my dismay, I had been refused under the condition stated by my superior, that my mother, "would be no less deceased upon your scheduled return in one month's time." I crumpled the letter furiously, casting it into the sputtering fireplace. How could he be so callous to a simple request? My anger was quickly tempered when I heard the constant footfalls above me cease. For a moment, I paused. I had grown so accustomed to them that their absence was unsettling. My ears strained against the rain outside as I thought I heard a whisper.

It was as though whatever, or whoever, had been running through the attic above me had found something to consider. As though there was much hushed discussion. I sat fearfully in silence and listened. When I finally decided that the stress had simply gotten the better of me and stood to go to bed, the voices stopped. Had it all been in my head? Or had my rustling paused their contemplation? As I drifted off to sleep, on the very edge of dreaming, I could just barely hear the whispering resume.

This pattern continued for a time. For how long I cannot remember, as the days bled into one another, and I was happy enough for it. I had resigned to finish out my stay here, for as heartless as my employer may be, I still had a house and a wedding to pay for back home. I would allow whatever was conspiring in the attic to go about its business as long as it allowed me to do the same. This new agreement seemed to work for us. I went about my daily tasks as dispassionately and disconnected as an automaton, then returned home in the evening and listened to the whispers in the attic. With each passing night, I could hear the secrets with more fidelity and clarity. With every hour I lay sleepless in my bed, staring at the ceiling, I deciphered another line of this inscrutable code. Then, the third letter arrived.

This one again from my betrothed. Inside was a short, impersonal letter informing me that my belongings would be removed from our home and sent to my mother's estate for collection at my earliest convenience. Included was the small diamond band for which I had saved my modest wages for months. As it turned out, my supervisor was tending to more than just my professional affairs. To my surprise, I laughed. Not the hearty laugh heard in joyous company, but the thin and strained laugh found only at the end of things. As I read the lines again and again, my laughter mixed with welling tears. What else could I do? Nothing mattered anymore. I had no reason to stay any longer. I would simply pack my things and leave at first light. As I lifted my eyes from the page, a chill colder than my resolve ran through me. I was certain I saw the shadow of a figure in the bedroom doorway. Just as soon as it appeared, it was gone. But the fear and dreadful curiosity remained and propelled me to investigate.

With candle in hand, I crept down the hallway toward the bedroom. Only a misshapen straw mattress, a small side table, and my travelling trunk furnished the chamber. Gazing around the room by candlelight and moonlit window, I followed the water-stained walls like a river up towards the ceiling. There sat the hatch into the attic. What could lie beyond those worn wooden boards? How my mind raced to fill in every dark and dismal terror that might await me in the confines above. With a trembling hand, I pushed open the hatch, inching ever so slowly. Assured that with every movement, some spectral fiend or maddened delinquent would reach out and seal my ill-fated end. Still, I pressed on. I had to know what terror was lurking above me all this time. The candle flame flickered as I crested the barrier. There in the empty, cobwebbed attic, the wind whistled through a rotten window, gently rapping the shutter against the night.

The Man in Red

by Dalainey Gervais

It's the second time the shed caught fire. Peering through the small window of the attic that faced the back of the property, The Intruder ponders on what to do, now that he has found refuge. His tip-toed pacing across the floors can only go on so long, as a family lives just below. Turning to the works of art adorning the loft wall, The Intruder admires the painting of a Man in Red.

Adorned with a crown made of thorns, beads of blood roll down the Man in Red's face, blending with his tears as they reach his sorrowful eyes. The Intruder admires the details of the eyes and follows their gaze to the attic window. During The Intruder's admiration of the painting, someone extinguished the fire that had taken over the shed. *They caught it just in time*, The Intruder thought to himself, noticing the fire has not left a trace on the shed's exterior.

The attic darkens as the sun sets and The Intruder finds himself wandering the room for a place to sleep. He lies at the foot of the painting of the Man in Red and falls into a deep slumber.

***

Awakened by the tinted orange of fire, The Intruder sprints to the little attic window to see the shed enveloped in flames for a third time. Unfazed, The Intruder looks to the Man in Red for comfort.

Rubbing the sleep out of his eyes, The Intruder notices the gaze of the painting's eye to be different than he remembered. He was sure the painting was looking out through the window the night before. Now, the Man in Red is looking directly at him.

Having forgotten why he chose this attic as his refuge and feeling reassured by the presence of the Man in Red, The Intruder looks back to the burning shed. Noticing the clouds collecting in anger, The Intruder braces himself for the worst. Bolts of lightning strike the shed, and thunder rattles through the house. Curiously, the quaint neighborhood doesn't worry about the burning shed or worsening weather as an early morning dog walker strolls past the apocalyptic scene. With the crashing of lightning, the attic window splinters to the floor. Turning to shield himself from the glass, The Intruder notices the eyes of the painting following him. Panicked, The Intruder begs the Man In Red for refuge.

"Protect me from the storm," he pleads. "Take pity on me, and my soul will be yours."

The Man In Red reaches out from the painting, putting a hand on The Intruder's shoulder.

"Follow my light," he says. Calmed by the reassurance from the painting, The Intruder makes his way to the door, which leads to the rest of the house. Enveloped by a spirit, The Intruder goes down the narrow stairs and finds his way into the living room. Blinded by the light protruding from the fire of the shed, The Intruder walks by framed pictures covered in dust, depicting himself and a family that once was. He was never an intruder but the man of this dwelling. Ignoring the relics of his forgotten past, The Intruder makes his way out of the lonely house and into the imagined burning shed.

A group of men sitting around a table greet The Intruder, with the Man in Red sitting among them. The Intruder sits to the left of the Man in Red, who offers him bread and wine. Smiling in spite of the flames engulfing him, The Intruder accepts his final meal.

***

Years later, the home stays untouched, collecting dust. Neighbours peer at the house, wondering whether its owner, The Hermit, would ever be seen again. Tales of The Hermit are told amongst the children, who suspect a curse took over him. Legend says an enchanted figure took what was left of his hope, leading him to madness. After all, he saw flames nobody else did. Unbeknownst to the neighborhood, The Hermit's corpse had been sitting, collecting dust in the shed. Or perhaps, he had been pecked at by wild animals. Maybe even by the Man In Red he proclaimed to have taken pity over his lost soul. We can only speculate about his fate until we meet our own.

The End, a Beautiful Day

by Edwin M. W. Smith

Jeremy stands alone in the kitchen of a dark, powerless house while his wife lies resting nearby. A piercing silence fills the room, and the faint tick of an old clock is all he has to drown out the sound of his own heart beating.

Everything that once existed outside has faded from Jeremy's memory, and the house has become his universe. It's a strange universe where seconds feel like hours and where hours rush past in the blink of an eye. A dizzying universe, where the floor rocks like a boat and everything is in constant motion around him. But more than anything, it's an infertile universe.

Starvation's sting has become easier to bear with time, yet it still leeches away at his strength like weighted chains, bound to his body and mind. Even the most basic of tasks are getting harder with each passing day, and it's only a matter of time before survival will become impossible.

Just focus on today, Jeremy, he reminds himself.

One of his eyes goes partially blind. This has happened before, but it has never lasted more than a few minutes. Though it still feels uncomfortable, so he closes that eye.

He leans forward over the fake marble countertop and, with his one good eye, stares into a small window covered by a thin sheet.

Only here does sunlight illuminate the shadowy interior of the house. It feels strange to be out of the darkness, yet comforting—warm even.

For a moment, Jeremy shuts his eyes, trying to recall what the view once looked like. The colour red comes to mind—a patch of tulips, perhaps, or a lone cherry tree. The ground is a shade of green, but the details are not there—and the sky is but a gigantic wall of blue stretching upwards forever. Everything has a yellow tint.

He opens his eyes to the sight of light being ripped out of the room and nearly screams at the sight.

As fast as possible, Jeremy drops to the floor and pushes himself up against the cabinets. *Shit, shit, shit.* He covers his mouth to muffle panicked breaths and braces himself for the house to start shaking violently.

He can only hope Evelyn stays where she is, lest she's killed by debris.

The room fills back up with light after a few seconds, and Jeremy, still panicked, sits up.

He looks up at the clock made from wood and brass, with a glass plate over its face. Its swinging pendulum is hard to see with his poor vision, but the weight is clear as it hovers motionless mid-fall.

There are markings clearly visible on the glass plate for the hour hand, which Jeremy had placed there when all of this had just started. They divide the clock into intervals of various lengths; half of them are labelled *safe*, whilst the rest say *hide*. Right now, the clock is still well within the safe range.

Jeremy groans in frustration, knowing how much energy it will take to stand back up, and all for a false alarm. "Stupid clouds," he mutters to himself.

Grabbing hold of the counter's ledge, he slowly pulls himself up. However, both legs are practically numb, refusing to hold him up. And as Jeremy tries to force them to do otherwise, he becomes increasingly nauseous and dizzy. Eventually, he's forced to stop and rest on top of the counter.

Being dehydrated and unable to sweat, he pants until his breath becomes cool on his tongue. "Don't faint," he tells himself, forcing himself to focus on something small until the nausea and dizziness goes away. One of the thin metal handles across from him does the trick.

As soon as everything goes back to normal, Jeremy notices that he's been staring at the pantry. He grunts in embarrassment, realizing he was supposed to get the rations. He laughs from exhaustion and lightheadedness, while internally crying in frustration at his inability to remember anything.

Jeremy stumbles over to the pantry and grabs hold of its two handles for support.

Inside are bags of dry lentils and beans; stale pasta; half a bag of rice; an empty bin where onions and potatoes were once stored; and various cans. Most of this stuff is unusable without a working stove, and it would be too dangerous to start a fire, even if it was done in a metal pot.

Jeremy grabs a can of baked beans at random, then drags himself towards the cutlery drawers to rummage around in search of a can opener.

Everything looks the same to his tired and disoriented eyes, making it near impossible to find anything. *Come on, where is it?* He tries to slam the drawer closed in frustration, but it's slam-proof; this only serves to irritate him even more.

After several minutes, he looks up to see the can opener still lying on the counter from yesterday. Fighting the urge to throw it against the wall, he opens the can and fishes out the sharp metal cover.

He stumbles towards a garbage bin placed off to the side and throws the cover inside. Then, with the open can in one hand, he slowly makes his way back to Evelyn.

He stumbles through a dark hallway and into an equally dark room.

Inside, Evelyn is lying across a couch with a blanket over her feet, with a generic landscape photo hanging across from her.

Evelyn silently stares at the image as Jeremy sits down near her head.

"I have the rations," he says.

She sits up and rests her head on his shoulder.

"Here," he says, handing her the open can.

She holds it for a few seconds, then hands it back to him. "I'm not hungry," she says quietly.

"You haven't eaten since yesterday."

"I'm fine; I'll... I'll eat later."

Jeremy puts the can to his mouth and eats half of it before putting the remains on a side table. "You've been staring at that image all day."

"I just like looking at the sky; the blue feels good on my eyes."

Jeremy puts his arms around Evelyn and holds her close.

"Hey Jeremy," says Evelyn.

"Yeah."

"The tap still doesn't work, right?"

"Yeah. We still have those giant plastic bottles in the basement, though."

"And how many do we have left?"

"Four."

She sighs. "I'm tired."

"I can get you your pillow."

"No, not like that. I'm tired of this, of everything. The limited food, the darkness, not being able to look outside—it's all horrible."

"We can't leave this place, you know that."

"Why not? We're gonna die either way."

"We'll live much longer in here."

"Still, I don't want this miserable place to be our grave." Evelyn unwraps her blanket and begins to stand up.

Jeremy quickly stands to hold her up and goes blind. "Not again." He holds his hand out to feel his way to a bookshelf placed near the room's door. *How am I still stumbling?* he asks himself, unable to comprehend how, despite being in near-constant darkness, blindness is still such a hindrance.

Evelyn guides his hand to the shelf.

"Thanks."

"No problem; but this is the exact thing I'm talking about. How many times a day have you been going blind?"

"I don't remember."

She sighs. "How long are we gonna live like this?" asks Evelyn.

"I... I don't know. Maybe forever."

She chuckles. "Ain't that a fantasy." She stumbles out of the room the way a drunkard might leave a bar, barely balanced and incapable of walking straight.

"Wait!" He comes to Evelyn's side and holds her up by her armpit.

She pushes his arm away. "I'm fine. Don't waste your energy."

Jeremy stands still as his wife makes her way to the front door. "Where are you going?"

"For a walk."

Jeremy limps towards her. "Don't go."

"You don't have to stay behind." She hooks her arm around Jeremy's and pulls him to the entrance. "Come on, I want to see the flowers." She reaches for the handle, stiff from unuse.

"I don't want to die."

"You'll have to face death sooner or later, and starvation isn't a pleasant way to go out."

The doorknob clicks as it breaks free from the notch in the frame. And, as a gentle breeze blows the door open, light bursts in and floods the entire house in a split second.

"Come on," she continues, "walk with me."

Jeremy begrudgingly says, "Okay," and the two of them make their way outside.

Hide and Seek

by Amy Lawford

I have just finished my shift at the St. James Hospital for sick kids. My feet are swollen and aching from my latest twelve-hour shift. Working as a nurse keeps me terribly busy and often leaves me making my way home in the dead of night. The bus pulls up and I clamber on, taking the last available seat in the rear. The heat is blasting and before I know it, the rhythmic movements of the bus have rocked me to sleep.

I'm jarred awake by the sound of the driver's booming voice. "Last stop, Miss," he bellows from the driver's seat.

Disoriented, I open my eyes and panic as I realize I have no idea where I am. I gather my belongings and begrudgingly disembark from the bus. It's a cold, dark night. The moon is hidden under a thick blanket of clouds. The air is chilly and nips at my nose and cheeks. I've never been to this part of town before. The houses that line the street look old, shabby, and abandoned. I rifle through my purse for my phone, thinking I can call a cab to take me home. Damn, it's dead. I forgot to charge it at work. I look up and down the street and notice a house with a dim light blinking through one of the windows. Creepy. I cross the street, walk towards the house, and take a deep breath before climbing the four broken steps that lead to the front door. It's an old oak door, painted black. The paint is chipping away, and the door looks like it's rotting. There is a big brass knocker ... it's so heavy I barely manage to lift it up. *Boom.* *Boom.* I hear the echo of my knock flow through the inside of the house. The door creaks open a foot, and my nose is filled with the smell of decay.

"Hello? Anyone home?" No answer. "I'm sorry to bother you, but I was hoping to use your phone." No answer. I walk inside. There is a large fireplace on the wall to my right and its flickering fire must have been the light I saw from the street. "Hello?" I call again.

I hear the floors creak from another room and a faint, feminine voice giggles and says, "Hi." Relieved that someone is home, I walk towards the voice.

"I'm so sorry to bother you, but I'm lost and was hoping I could use your telephone to call a cab." I hear another giggle. The front door makes a large groaning sound as it slams shut. Startled, I let out a loud gasp. Another giggle.

"Sorry, we don't have a phone." The voice is the same but hearing it a second time makes me think that it must be a little girl.

"Are your parents home?" I ask, my voice betraying my lack of confidence.

"No, they are gone," the voice answers me.

I hear footsteps running across the floor and moving in my direction. I look towards the sound and see a little girl. She cannot be more than five years old. She has long dark hair and is wearing a pink polka dot dress that is visibly dirty and ripped at the knees.

"Wanna play a game?" the little girl asks me. She smiles at me, exposing a row of small, yellow teeth.

"Are you all alone? Who lives here with you?" I ask. She giggles and runs away from the fire and back into the darkness. Something does not feel right. Not just the little girl, but the whole house. The house has a spooky vibe, and I don't like it. I feel my blood curdling inside of me. The hair on my arms stands up. Goosebumps run down my spine. I back up slowly, making my way back towards the front door.

"Where are you going?" the small voice asks me. "Don't you wanna play a game, Mary Beth?" I feel a rush of panic flow through my body. I'm not wearing my name tag.

"How do you know my name?" I ask, still moving towards the door.

"You told me, silly." More giggling. I try to replay the last two minutes in my mind. Did I say my name when I knocked and asked for the phone? I can't remember. I must have. I feel the door against my back now. I turn and grab the knob, pulling it hard. Nothing happens. It won't open.

"Do you like hide and seek?" the little girl asks me. I can't figure out where she is. The whole house is black, except for the light from the fire. I pull on the door a few more times. Still nothing.

"It's locked," the little girl says. I hear her running back and forth in the darkness. "Stay and play a game with me and I'll open it." She giggles. I stand frozen, too scared to move, too scared to answer. "I'll go first. You count to ten, then come and find me," she whispers. I do not move. I do not answer. "If you don't play then I will get upset," she says to me in a whiny voice.

"If I find you, will you unlock the door for me?" I ask, my voice trembling.

"Mmhmm," I hear her answer.

I start to count aloud, "one, two, three" then "eight, nine, ten. Ready or not here I come," I yell. Fuck. I cannot see anything and the last thing I want to do is walk further into this house. I take a few cautious steps forward. Silence. Only the crackle of the fire. I have my hands out in front of me, reaching in the dark. I feel the wall on my left. I follow it forward. My foot hits a step. *Stairs,* I think to myself. I hear the patter of feet running above me.

"You'll never find me," I hear her laugh with a squealing excitement in her voice. I lift my foot onto the first step, counting as I climb. "You'll never get out." The giggling continues and gets louder the higher I step. I stop at number 12. There are 12 steps.

Realizing I am now at the top, I try and focus my eyes. I cannot see a thing. No shapes, no outlines. Just black. I slowly take a step forward. I move my arms in the dark, hoping to find a wall. Nothing. Another step forward. I feel disoriented. My hand hits something solid. What is it? A door. I keep walking forward, through the door. The smell. It fills my nostrils. I know that smell. I have experienced it before. At the hospital. Death. I can barely swallow. My mouth is dry and it's hard to take a breath.

"Getting warmer," she says to me. I can hear the excitement in her voice. I take three more steps and I am inside a room. I still cannot make anything out. Only the smell. My hands drop to the floor as I try and guide myself further. I feel the rough floorboards under my palms. I feel the base of what I think is a bed frame. I use the frame to pull myself up so that I am standing. I hear her giggle. She is close.

"You're burning hot," she yells. I move my hand along the side of the bed, walking forward. I feel the soft fabric of a blanket brush against my hand. I reach forward, pulling the blanket away from the bed. "You found me!" she shouts with excitement. My hands search in the darkness. There is something lying on the bed. I reach out, my heart beating in my chest. No. It's a small lump on the bed. I feel around some more. Bone. I can feel bones. I scream. "Don't be scared, Mary Beth. It's your turn to hide. I'll find you."

It was not a little girl's voice.

The Search for Nothing

by Nicholas Saumur

All I wanted was to be alone. It was for that reason, to escape from the burdens of society, that I had moved to the country, far from civilization. I despised the loud noises and people. Oh, how I despised the people. It had been a month since I had moved to this place. I just had to get away from those stuffy, polluted cities.

If you are reading this, you have no doubt seen my ancient house, with its crumbling stonework and antique furniture. And with no doubt you found my laboratory in the basement with the walls covered in complex machines. I had always considered myself a man of science, studying the mysteries of the universe for the betterment of mankind. My father was a doctor, and his father was a physicist, so science ran in my family. I was no exception. I wanted to make a discovery so great that I would become rich, buy a mansion, and block out the outside world. But what would this discovery be?

Black holes have always perplexed us, but if I could create one and find some use for it, my name would be in the history books forever.

***

It was late one night, what date it was I do not know, when I made a rather shocking discovery. I will not go into the details of my experiment for fear of someone replicating it. I created a floating orb about a foot in diameter. It was transparent at first, but soon turned pitch black, and from there my descent into misery and madness began.

I started with small rodents. I tied them to tethers, threw them in and waited. They always came out safe and sound, no matter how long I put them in. The longest time I put a mouse in was for 72 hours. It showed no signs of dehydration or hunger, leading me to conclude that the energy had a suspended animation effect.

Over the course of many months, I tried to make the orb as large as possible so that I could enter it. Over long sleepless nights, I toiled away, performing countless experiments. Occasionally, I thought I could hear whispers coming from within the sphere, but I simply dismissed it as a result of my lack of sleep. I grew more and more distant from the outside world. My poor father passed away during my experiments. When I received the letter, I merely ignored it and threw it in the trash. At the time I had simply considered it as a minor distraction.

Then, after 8 months, my hard work had finally paid off. I found a way to generate enough energy to make the sphere large enough for me to slip through. I fastened a thick tether to my waist, and attached it to a winch that was in turn attached to the concrete wall of my cellar. I had a mechanism that would pull me back in the event of mortal danger. However, I considered this precaution unnecessary, for I assumed I had nothing to fear.

I was filled with pride at my accomplishment. I was about to do something that no man had ever done before. I plunged into the sphere and was greeted by cool air. I immediately felt weightless as I floated in the empty void. There was an unearthly silence, and it was so dark it was as if I was blind. I felt at peace here in this place. No one could bother me here; I was finally, truly alone.

Five minutes in, I started to hear the whispers. They were incomprehensible and made me feel uneasy. I was about to return to my laboratory when something grabbed my ankle and started to pull me down. It was followed by a dozen more, grabbing at my legs. I flipped the switch that activated the mechanism that started to pull me free. The unearthly hands grasped and pulled harder, my captors (or perhaps captor?) would not let me go so easily. In a desperate struggle, I tried pulling myself up the cable, but was of no use.

My strength was failing, and freedom seemed impossible. That's when I could see something in the dark. It was darker than my surroundings, but I could not discern any other details. It was formless, it seemed infinitely large, and as it approached the whispers grew louder. I doubled my efforts to stop this thing from catching me, and was rewarded with an intense pain in my leg as flesh tore itself apart.

I returned to my earthly plane and came crashing down to the floor. Despite the pain of my bloody stump I was clutching, I was relieved to be back in my home. That feeling was soon replaced with dread.

It did not take me long to realize that everything was covered in a thick layer of dust. All my machines were falling apart, and the room was only lit by moonlight shining through a narrow window at the back of the room. I theorized that time moves slower in that place than here, which is why I found my laboratory in a state of disrepair. My thoughts were confirmed when I found 50 years' worth of mail had been slid through my mail slot.

My crippled leg was not much of a problem, thanks to the teachings of my father I had considered useless to my profession until now. Once all of the chaos had subsided, the weight of my situation began to set in. I was still alone. Everyone I had known was likely dead. There was no one who could help me.

As I sat in my study trying to think of what I could do, I began to hear the whispers again. I hoped it was nothing, but as the night wore on, I began to see dark shapes in the corner of my vision.

I knew that thing would come for me soon, so I began preparations to abandon my house, but I was stopped by a horrid realization. What if I had unleashed this force upon the world and nowhere was safe?

With that in mind, I set about with my final experiment. Using what I had learned from the creation of the orb, I focused the dark energies outward onto the house to ensure nothing could ever escape.

***

My house is now an infinite labyrinth; a maze of repeating rooms. I have finally found the peace I had sought. If someone is here and reading this tale I apologize. I know not if there is an escape from this prison, for I have not sought one out. This is my punishment. I accept it willingly.

In my final hours, I know that it will not be long before the thing finds me, and perhaps you as well.

Ignition

Knowing others is intelligence; knowing yourself is true wisdom. Mastering others is strength; mastering yourself is true power.
— Lao Tzu

Rot

by Jack Dingwall

Elizabeth was walking through the woods on her way home from work when she came across a rotting corpse. It was lying in the shadows of the tree line, just off the forest trail. Elizabeth looked at it with pity, observed its filthy, torn clothes, its matted hair, its blackened teeth. And the corpse spoke to her.

I am in need, it hissed. *These bones do not belong here in the mud and the muck. Bugs crawl into my eye sockets, and maggots eat at my flesh. I would like to once again be granted the dignity of resting in a house. Please, this I beg of you.*

Elizabeth continued to stare at the poor thing. She thought of her own house, so big and empty, with drafty windows and floorboards that never seemed to settle. Maybe they would both be comfortable this way. She stooped low and scooped the corpse up in both of her arms, carrying it down the path as if it were her bride.

When they arrived at her house, she gently placed it on the front step so she could unlock her door. Inside was Elizabeth's kitchen, small but well stocked. Beyond the kitchen, the house opened up to a grand living room with tall standing lamps, a plush carpet, and a large cushy armchair sitting by a fireplace. It was in this chair that Elizabeth placed the corpse before bending down to light a fire.

As the warm glow began to fill the room, Elizabeth returned to the corpse, slumped over and slack-jawed in its chair. She pushed its torso up, so it sat in a reclining position. She closed its mouth, so it looked a little less ridiculous. Then, as an afterthought, she picked up its right leg, crossed it over the left one, and placed its hands on its lap.

Thank you. Your kindness and understanding have given me peace that I have not known in quite some time. But, now that I am resting in a chair, in a house, I am feeling much as I did when I was alive. I am quite hungry. Might you have some food to spare for this poor old bag of bones?

Elizabeth stopped for a second to consider. She had plenty of food, and she loved to cook, but what's the use in cooking for a corpse? How could its rotted taste buds enjoy anything they encountered over the taste of death? Eventually, she made her way over to the fridge and dug out of the back a punnet of raspberries that were starting to look a little squishy anyway.

She brought them back to the corpse hesitantly, unsure how to go about it. She slowly reached one hand out to the corpse's face and opened its jaws once more. Then, she grabbed a handful of berries and gently placed them in the corpse's mouth. As soon as the berries touched its teeth, it came alive, devouring them with nothing less than unrestrained ferocity.

Elizabeth made to pull her hand away but before she could, the corpse grabbed her wrist tightly. It brought her hand back to its mouth, and its swollen tongue began to lap at her fingers, licking away any remaining juice and pulp from the berries. When it was satisfied, it let go of Elizabeth and dropped its hand to its side, inert once again.

I thank you for the second time. I am quite tired. I will rest now.

And so, it sat there silently.

Elizabeth, feeling rather overwhelmed by it all, climbed the wooden steps that led upstairs and went straight to bed.

The next day, when Elizabeth awoke, she went straight down to check on the corpse. It was sitting in its chair in the same position she had left it in the night before. She eyed it cautiously, as if it might come alive again, but it just sat there. Then she noticed that the chair beneath it had changed; there was a large dark splotch right underneath the corpse, as if the chair was rotting.

She got to work making breakfast, eggs and bacon. No sooner than the food started to bubble and sizzle in the pan, the corpse spoke up again.

Is that food you are making, my dear?

"Yeah," she called back, "just my breakfast."

It looks so delicious. Would you mind terribly if I partook as well?

Elizabeth looked down at the eggs and bacon in her pan, made just how she liked them. She sighed. She dumped them out onto a plate and retrieved a fork, walking over to the corpse. This time, she knew what to expect when she put the first bit of egg into its mouth. It chewed so carelessly that it kept crunching down on the fork as well. Once the last piece of bacon was gone, Elizabeth went to make herself more, expecting the corpse to remain idle now that it had eaten.

She had just cracked a new egg into the pan when it spoke again.

More.

"Excuse me?"

More, I need more.

Elizabeth stared at the food. She was hungry. But she served up another round of food anyway. That couldn't satisfy the corpse either. The corpse kept demanding food until there were no eggs and bacon left at all. It asked what else was in the fridge. Each food item she named, it demanded for itself. Leftover pasta, unopened quarts of yogurt, luncheon meats, a stick of butter. As it ate, the dark rot beneath it began to grow, working its way down the chair and into the floor below it. Once the fridge was empty, it asked about the pantry. Elizabeth's stomach was growling with hunger, but she knew the corpse had gone without food much longer than she. So, she continued to feed it cans of tuna, tomato soup, a jar of peanut butter. The corpse downed all of it with the same disregard for decorum.

Finally, the corpse had just finished licking the last drops of a jar of honey when it once again wailed *more, MORE,* and Elizabeth was forced to say, "But there isn't any more. You ate all of it." The corpse was silent for a long moment. Elizabeth was beginning to think it had settled down again; maybe it was satisfied. But it had more to ask of her.

Please my dear, after all those days sprawled so uncomfortably across the forest floor, I grew so very sore. I think if I were to simply have a hot bath, I would feel so much more like myself again.

Wearily, Elizabeth pushed her hunger aside and went upstairs to draw a bath with steaming water. She retrieved the corpse and was very careful not to bump its head as she brought it up to the bathroom. Gently, she laid it down in the tub. She turned the spout off and left to give it some privacy.

Back downstairs, Elizabeth spent a second examining the rot coming from the corpse's chair. It had expanded, surrounding the chair, breaking down the living room carpet. It stank too, the smell of death thick in the air like a relentless fog. As she was examining, it grew even more, expanding outwards right before her eyes. It wouldn't be long before there was no living room carpet left. Elizabeth didn't know what to do.

In the kitchen, there were drops and bits of food on the floor from her rush to get it all to the corpse's mouth. She fished a rag out of the cupboard under her sink and began wiping the food away. She went back to the sink to wash the rag off but, when she turned the water on, the liquid that came out was as black as ink and carried the same rotting stench that the corpse was spreading all over her house.

With an inkling of what the problem might be, Elizabeth ran back upstairs as fast as she was able. She burst into the bathroom to find the corpse sitting in a tub full of the repulsive, black water. Pushing down her nausea, she plunged her arms into the mire and wrapped them around the corpse's torso. She heaved its now waterlogged body out and slung it over her shoulder.

As she carried it downstairs, she saw the rot that had taken over her living room was now spreading through the pipes, leaving veins of foul grime crisscrossing across her walls, fattening by the second.

She stumbled down the last few steps and dragged the bloated corpse back to the husk of her living room so she could throw it into what was left of the armchair. She stood staring at the corpse, wondering how she could have let it go this far. She was just so lonely. And the corpse had looked so sad. She couldn't help but give it everything it asked for. And, of course, it asked for more.

Cold. I grow cold. The first night I was here, you so lovingly lit a fire for me. Do you think you would be able to light it once more?

Elizabeth wasn't even sure she could. All the firewood was rotted, and the fireplace had sunken in on itself, crumpled like a discarded wrapper. But she placed new logs where she could squeeze them in and struck a match. To her surprise, it caught almost instantly. The corpse let out a noise, like a contented sigh, though Elizabeth could feel no heat coming from the fire. Elizabeth collapsed onto the decomposing floor, hungry, exhausted, and soaking wet. She lay there, staring up at her ceiling as her house wasted away around her.

My dear, spoke the corpse, *it has been so long since my last meal. I feel hunger gnawing at my stomach even now. If you could spare som-*

"I don't have any," said Elizabeth, sitting up to look the corpse in the eye. "I have no more food."

Well, in that case, might I have som-

"I don't have *anything*. There is nothing here for you anymore. You took everything."

The corpse seemed to consider this. It sat still for a moment. Then, abruptly, it stood up and walked out of the house at a strange, jerking pace. On spindly, shaking limbs it walked back down the path and into the forest, leaving Elizabeth and her house behind. She didn't have the energy to chase after it, or to call out to it. She didn't even have the energy to stand up. She just sat there, on her living room floor, and waited for the rot to consume her as well.

Filling Your Purse

by Becca Nicholson

To my sister, Fiona. We both deserve to put ourselves first.

Every morning before heading out the door, Lexie packs up her purse; a midsized purple bag with a simple, floral design. She keeps all sorts of items in there, from Band-Aids and tissues to loose change and chewing gum. Lexie looks through the purse and decides what she needs throughout the day. Every morning, the purse is filled to the brim as she goes to work.

As she walks into the office one Thursday, her co-worker Mark comes scurrying up to her.

"Hey Lex, any chance you have some gum on you? I've got a meeting in 10 minutes." She pulls out a pack of gum and hands a piece to Mark. He eyeballs the pack. "Can I grab a few? Never know when you need them," he says, eyes darting between her and the conference room. She obliges and pulls out a few more sticks. Mark nods his head and dashes towards his meeting. Lexie continues to her desk.

As she goes to sit down, another co-worker, Margie, approaches, her nose a bright red.

"Hey, Lex," she says, sounding stuffed up. "I really need some tissues. I've got a cold, but I've got that meeting with Hanna I can't miss. Got a pack?" Lexie pulls the pack out of her purse, and Margie snatches it from her hand. "Ugh, thank god." Margie turns away, and Lexie turns back to her desk, shoulders slumped.

As the day progresses, more people ask her for different things. Her co-worker Lucas comes up, holding his phone.

"Hey! My phone is dead. Can I borrow your charger?" She hands it over, hoping this time he remembers to bring it back before the end of the day. At lunch, Carlos and Mia, both ask her for some change.

"We really need a coffee today, Lex." She empties her change purse into their hands as they set out towards the Starbucks. After lunch, Vanessa asks if Lexie has any snacks in her purse.

"I had to skip out on lunch today, but I knew you'd have something." Lexie hands over her granola bar. Over and over, people walk up to Lexie's desk and ask her for things, and just as she does every day, she opens her purse for them.

The day winds down, and yet people continue to ask Lexie for more. Hanna walks up to her, looking ill.

"I think Margie gave me her cold! You got any lozenges?" Lexie hands them over and begins packing up when her boss walks up to her desk.

"Hey Lexie, great work today. I'm heading out soon. Would you mind staying a little late? We can't pay you for the overtime, but I was hoping you wouldn't mind … it's only about a half hour of extra work." His eyes widen slightly, as if trying to garner sympathy. Lexie can tell that he hopes she will say yes, because if not he will have to do the work himself. She looks at the ground.

"Yeah, I can do that."

Her boss smiles. "Great! Also, would you mind if I borrowed your umbrella? I know you usually bus home, so I figured it would be no big deal." Lexie hesitates, so her boss adds, "You know I'm not used to the Seattle rain yet. I haven't been here long enough!" Lexie sighs internally. He had arrived at the Seattle office around the same time as her. Eventually, she reaches into her purse and hands it over. He nods and puts the umbrella under his arm. "See you tomorrow, Lexie!" he says as he walks away. She looks outside and sees rain beating against the large windows of the office building.

Lexie finishes her extra work and then begins to pack up her stuff. She heads down to the bus stop, but as it pulls up, she realises that she gave away all her change. She waves the bus away and pulls out her phone, convincing herself that it's fine if she orders an Uber, just this once. The screen doesn't light up, and she remembers that Lucas never gave back the charger. Defeated, she begins the walk home. In the distance, she can see the Space Needle through the rain. Her intention was to visit this weekend, but she knows that her phone call tonight may change those plans.

The rain begins to pick up, and without the umbrella she gave away, Lexie is forced to pull her coat above her head. The winds around her swirl as she's pulled in different directions. The rain beats down heavily on her back, and she takes shelter under an awning nearby, desperate for some refuge from the rainstorm. She searches her purse for something to wipe the rain from her face until she remembers she gave away her pack of tissues to Margie. She instead wipes her face on her sleeve and continues.

By the time she reaches her apartment, the weight of her soaked clothes pulls her down, making her body feel heavy. Exhausted, she pulls open the door and peels off the drenched clothing, layer by layer. She places the empty purse onto her velvet green couch and plugs her phone into her extra charger. She puts on her favourite t-shirt and a pair of sweatpants. She refills her cat's food dish then goes back to sit on her bed. Watching as her phone screen lights up, Lexie sees them. Two missed calls. It's 7:48 pm now, long after the first call came through, and she knows it's going to cause an issue. The phone starts to ring again. She watches it ring once, twice, three times before she picks up.

"Hi, Mom."

"Well now Alexia, why would you keep me waiting? Every day I call at the same time. You should know when to pick up!" Her mother sighs. "Alexia, you need to come home this weekend to take care of your sisters. Your father and I are trying to go to your cousin's cabin."

Lexie's shoulders slump. "Mom, I don't know if I can this weekend..." she murmurs, already knowing her mother won't take no for an answer.

"Alexia. Your father and I sacrificed so much for you; the least you can do is come take care of your sisters while we make up for the time we lost taking care of you."

Lexie's body stiffens. She hangs her head low, unable to think of anything to say. She knows how much her parents gave up. They never miss an opportunity to tell her. She knows it's her turn to help them now. She has to do everything she can to help them.

"Alright, Mom, I'll take the train up to your house Friday night."

Her mom lets out a satisfied humph. "Well, at least you aren't being ungrateful. We'll see you on Friday." She promptly hangs up.

Lexie puts the phone down next to her and falls back on her bed, exasperated. She feels inconsiderate for wanting a weekend to herself. She knows other people need her. It's selfish to even think about not helping others—she knows this. Her parents gave up so much to raise her. They sacrificed their youth for her. When her sisters were born, her parents guilted her into taking over the lion's share of their care. Since she moved out, there is hardly a weekend that she isn't taking the train back to help. She is exhausted and empty. She feels she has nothing left to give others. She gives every part of herself to others, never expecting anything in return. Eventually, they stopped offering.

She sits up, looking out the small window next to her bed. Her cat jumps up next to her and curls up in the bend of her legs. She watches as the rain hits the window next to her face, making a pitter-patter sound against the glass. In the distance, she sees the Space Needle standing proudly above the city. Despite living in Seattle for over a year, she has never been, though she has always wanted to go. She looks at her charging phone, thinking of the people in her life. Her co-workers, always taking what they need without so much as a thank you. Her parents, expecting her to drop everything for them. When was the last time she had done anything for herself?

She knows if she tries to back out of watching her sisters now, her mother will guilt her into it. They wouldn't be able to go to the cabin without her. They would have to deal with it on their own; something they have never done. Lexie watches the rain drops as they slowly make their way down the glass. Her hair is still damp from the walk home, and she curses herself for never being able to say no to anyone. She can't stand the idea of disappointing anyone, instead letting herself down. She is tired of it, and she knows the only way to take back her power is to let others deal with their own problems.

"If the pattern is to break," she says to herself out loud, "I have to be the one to break it."

On Saturday morning, she wakes up in her own bed, phone on airplane mode beside her. She goes about her daily routine, packing up her purse to get ready. Tissues, gum, some cash. She finishes packing up and heads out to grab the bus to the Space Needle. Today, everything in the bag is for her.

What You Missed

by Owen McDonald

The sun is down, and the wind holds a biting chill. You put your car in park, get out, and walk across a lot that could hold 50 cars but only contains 12. You've made this walk so many times over flat asphalt and towards a steeple you've been seeing since before you could read. It should be a place of normalcy, and it has been. But a lot has changed in the past 24 hours. The stagger in your steps betrays a trepidation that's new. Nevertheless, you reassure yourself, open the glass door, and step in.

There's nothing to surprise you inside. Not just because you come here all the time, but also because it looks like every other modern church. Rows of pews, some halls with rooms, and a foyer where the same people talk to the same people. None of that should be a problem for you. Mingling, socializing, small talk, and all those other things where some may fear stumbling are things you've always thrived in. But today, you're so tired and so sick with worry.

How many people know?

Before you've finished taking tabs on who's here, Andrew van Gilst is up in your face. In no time at all, he's corralling you through a conversation as dry as sun-bleached sand. You don't mind, though. The mundanity of it calms you, if only for a second. You'd think that as your pastor, Andrew would notice something wrong with you, but he just talks your ear off for two minutes before floating off to pester someone else. If your special talent is making people feel seen, then his is talking to everyone and noticing no one. Like a waterfall of worthless words, the man only pours out.

Standing there, abandoned by the semi-socializer, you see her and nearly retch. Alyson Lancaster, your girlfriend of three years. People always said she was wrong for you. Yesterday, she proved them right. You said some things are just for you, and Alyson disagreed. You dart past, hoping she won't notice.

She knows, but who has she told?

Distracted and flustered, you bump right into Harry Gilcrest. Harry isn't the kind of guy that gets along with everyone, but he gets along with you. Or he did. The two of you were inseparable in your senior year, crushing every other school with a hockey team. But now, "Don't touch me," are the only words he says to you as you're brushed off by one of your closest friends. The look of disgust on his face tells all. *He knows, and if he knows, they all do.*

You stand stunned in the center of the lobby. Harry and Alyson are talking. They're looking at you. Other people will do the same soon.

They Know. They Know. They Know.

You have to go. You have to go now! Sweating, heaving, and hyperventilating, it feels like hours before you finally move your feet, but it's only thirty seconds. You stumble to the glass double doors you just came from, and barrel out as I walk in. Your eyes, filling with tears, meet my own for the first time in years. Then, you're gone.

***

I'm told two days later. They don't say how, but the how doesn't matter. What matters is that you're gone. Gone forever. It doesn't feel real. When I overhear, when I'm told, I want to think it's some sick joke. I even laugh. Denial is a bitch.

But the funeral makes it real. The tears make it real. I guess I should be grateful that our parents stayed friends because otherwise, I wouldn't have been invited. I'm sitting so close. So close to where I last saw you. Why is goodbye a full week removed from then? Why is it always too late to say what we need to say?

How long ago was it? The last time we talked. The specifics are getting harder to remember. We were at yours. After school. In your room. Playing Xbox. At that moment, nothing seemed to matter, other than who would win. At least, that's what I've told myself ever since. But we both know it's a lie. You were trying to win the game while I was stealing glances at the side of your face.

We'd been friends for as long as I could remember, yet something had changed for me. I'd started thinking of you in a way I didn't want to, and I couldn't shut it out. A smile from you had once meant reassurance, then it meant I couldn't breathe. Sitting next to you was the most normal thing, then it wasn't. Then it took everything in me not to die inside when our legs so much as brushed together, and when they did, I know you saw the look on my face. So lonesome.

Is that why you pulled away? Why couldn't you admit that you felt the same?

We stopped talking when you started dating Alyson. She took the time that had been ours to share, and as life went on, I withered into a husk. There was no one else. More and more, I found I was just talking to myself. You were gone, but I spent all my hours thinking of you. In a way, I forced you to stay while forfeiting what little I still had.

People are whispering during your eulogy about things they never knew. They're saying that, in three years, you only ever kissed Alyson. Now she's told everyone why. She went digging through your room and found pictures of you. Pictures of me. Pictures of us. Now everyone knows the truth. You started dating her to hide who you really were, and she revealed it in the end. You threw it all away because of what they thought of you.

But I always knew, and I loved you.

Junior

by Rey Del R.

There once was a little village that held an annual contest that took place on the first day of fall. This event was a competition to see who could plant the tallest tree. Our story starts with Bradley, a young boy who has always wanted to plant a tree. He thinks to himself, *this year is going to be different! I know it is!*

As Bradley heads to the yard and looks around, he notices that there are more participants than ever. Each participant varies in age, ranging from his classmates to people as old as his grandmother.

"Rumour has it, the prize is gonna be bigger than last year's!" exclaims a passerby. Although that may be true, Bradley does not care about the prizes. As long as he has a tree by himself, it will all be worth it.

The announcer grabs everyone's attention and explains the contest.

"Alright ladies and gentlemen. The rules are very simple; all you need is a trowel and a watering can. Then plant the seed, and at the end of the year, whoever has the tallest tree wins a year's supply of pies!" Everyone shrugs in disappointment.

"A-and they're not just any ordinary pies, but we have made contact with the famous Michelin Star Chef herself, Mrs. Fields Berry!" Shocked, the crowd stops and gasps. Then they go wild. Mrs. Berry is a legendary baker who serves kings and is known to have the best pies across the land.

"That's right everybody! At New Year's, the village's guard will measure whose tree is the tallest. So let the competition ... begin!"

Many villagers rush in and start planting their seeds in the yard. Seeing how eagerly everyone buries their seeds, Bradley knows that this is going to be a challenge.

Once each villager plants their seed, they leave, hoping for their tree to grow. Bradley is sad that everyone is missing the main source of growth. He has a strategy in mind. They don't know that the secret to growing a strong tall plant is the power of love!

Bradley does what his mother taught him. He gently plants the seed, pats the dirt and says, "Hey there buddy! My name is Bradley, and you're in safe hands now. I know you'll grow to be big and strong." He smiles, rubs the ground, and gives it a kiss. "I love you."

Some of the villagers who have stayed look at him with disgust and whisper amongst themselves. Tyler, a boy the same age as Bradly, and from a wealthier family, comes over to him and picks on him saying...

"You'll never win the competition with something gross like that!" Tyler says, while looking disgusted. Tyler never does anything on his own. In fact, he always has someone else do his work for him. He boasts to everyone and says, "Ha ha! I'll be the winner this year, folks! Beware and behold my power, for I will have the tallest tree ever!"

Bradley doesn't listen to Tyler. Instead, he looks down to the ground where he buried his seed.

"Don't listen to him buddy, I believe we can win this. Imma call you Junior," he says to the seedling as he waters it.

***

Every day, people come, water their plants and leave. However not Bradley, he creates a routine. Every morning, at the same hour he talks to Junior. Tells it about his day, and compliments on how big it has gotten. Then he leaves for school and recites, "I know you'll grow big and strong! I love you, Junior," and kisses it. He continues to see Junior daily from dawn until dusk, and on days he's sick and can't go, he apologizes.

***

As fall ends, winter approaches, and the seedlings have already grown past their sapling stage. Bradley always thinks about Junior's safety: whether Junior would be alright, or if it's too cold. One day during school, as soon as the home bell rings, Bradley rushes straight to the door, only to be stopped by Tyler and his goons.

"Oh, look what we have here," says Tyler.

"It's the tree lover," says one of his goons.

"Are you meeting your friend again? You know that's not gonna get you far!" Tyler says mockingly.

"Let's push him around," says another of his goons.

They bully Bradley daily, picking on him because he has no friends. But that doesn't hinder Bradley, not in the slightest. Bradley's mom always told him that if you spread love and not hate, you will receive it in return. After his torment, he has no ill will towards them. If Junior is okay, then he is okay. After they leave, he heads straight towards the yard.

When Bradley arrives, he spots the guard on duty. *It's good to see a guard here to prevent acts of sabotage*, Bradley thinks to himself. The guard greets Bradley.

"Meeting Junior again?" asks the guard.

"Yes ma'am," answers Bradley.

She looks at him.

"Colour me impressed; I have never seen anyone put in this much effort to win."

"It's not always about winning, it's about how much love you've put into it." Bradley smiles.

28

The guard smiles and opens the gate for him. Bradley promises her a slice of pie if he wins, as thanks for watching Junior. He approaches what was once an empty field and is now a blooming space for trees. Some large, some thin, and some that are bending and swirling. But everyone's trees seem to be doing fine, and if you were to look at them, you would see that they're all about the same height. All but Tyler's, which is the tallest out of the bunch, and Junior, which is sadly the smallest of all. It isn't even the size of a regular tree. Bradley is not disturbed by this at all, he just thinks it is a slow grower. He approaches Junior with glee and says, "Just one more month Junior! Once you have finally grown you will not only become the tallest, but the greatest tree! Greater than anyone can imagine!" He continues to talk to Junior for the rest of the day, says his usual loving farewells and leaves the yard. He heads home and dreams about Junior.

***

There is only one day left until the new year, and all the villagers feel defeated. Tyler's tree is still by far the tallest at a whopping 25 metres tall, which also boosts his ego. Despite this, Bradley stands proud seeing Junior all grown up, though it is unfortunately short of Tyler's by five metres. He is still happy though. He had lots of fun talking and seeing Junior grow.

With ever-growing confidence, Tyler hops on top of a rock and says, "Everyone stand down, and don't bother trying, for all your trees are no match for mine! Especially that little, tiny tree over there; I heard its name is Junior," he says, pointing directly at Bradley to provoke him. "A fitting name for a tree that small." Some of the villagers giggle, but it doesn't bother Bradley at all.

Determined, Bradley approaches Tyler. Challenging him.

"Oh yeah, want to make a bet?" he says. The villagers stop laughing in shock. "If I win, I want you to apologize to me and Junior." Everyone laughs again in disbelief, despite Bradley looking unfazed.

"Oh, you're serious?" Tyler questions with a puzzled expression. "Well, fine, it's pointless anyways. You have no hope whatsoever. If I win, I want you to polish my shoes, deal?" Without hesitation, Bradley shakes Tyler's hand and thus seals the deal.

***

New Year's Eve comes along, and the stakes are high, with all the trees still looking the same. Bradley is now sitting in the yard, looking at Junior, concerned.

"Sorry I started this bet Junior, all I wanted was for Tyler to change. I don't want you to feel bad and plus, I'm good at shining shoes anyways!" He spends the rest of the day with Junior, in the snow. Bradley isn't cold at all, he just keeps talking to Junior for hours, right up until midnight.

Bradley tells Junior about how he never had friends and explains that Tyler was his first-ever friend. He assumed that Tyler started picking on him because of his lack of socializing. He starts to tear up.

29

"I just wanna be friends again." Then, fireworks light the night sky up, signalling the new year.

Bradley somberly wishes Junior a happy New Year, as Tyler laughs behind him while confidently approaching him.

"It's midnight, loser. Who still has the biggest tree? Oh yeah, it's me. Looks like I was right; there's no hope for you. You'll start in the morning. I want to look good in front of Mrs. Fields while you shine my shoe," Tyler says with a laugh before he is strutting away.

Bradley looks at his tree.

"Don't worry Junior, I'm still proud of you," He gets himself together, stands up, then kisses Junior for the last time and leaves after a big hug.

"Alright," says the guard as she approaches Bradley. "The bet is over. I need you to go to your home so I can lock the doors. So, no nefarious business." Bradley agrees to go home and heads straight to bed. Bradley hopes that Tyler won't be too harsh with his new job in the morning and falls asleep.

***

As sunrise comes, Bradley gets out of his bed, grabs his shoeshine kit and heads straight to the yard. As he leaves his house, he sees something that's unordinary. He's greeted by a big shadow in the sky. Bradley's eyes widen. He rushes to the yard and sees everyone looking up at the sky. Everyone is just as surprised as him. Though, looking at Tyler, he looked so shocked that his mouth was so open, a whole apple could fit inside.

Biggest is an understatement, and it is definitely not Tyler's.

With no contest, Junior towers above all, all the way through the clouds, with Tyler's tree coming in second.

"H-how? How can this be?" Tyler looks flabbergasted.

"Oh, *wow*, magnifique!" says the one and only famous baker as she arrives. "Eet looks like zee tallest tree I 'ave ever seen! Whose tree ees eet?"

"That tree is named Junior," replies Bradley with a smile.

"Junior ah? I 'ave never 'eard of someone naming a tree. An interesting name for somezing zat ees big. What's your secret?" Mrs. Fields asks.

Bradley giggles.

"Well, it's the power of love!"

Mrs. Fields' eyes widen.

"Zat's zee same way I make my pies!" she exclaims, as she smiles with excitement. "Congratulations Bradley, eet will be an 'onour for me to make pies for you."

The announcer speaks the results.

"You heard it here folks! The winner of this competition is ... Bradley!"

The villagers congratulate Bradley as he sees Tyler outside the crowd, looking down, tearing up a bit. He decides to approach him.

"What do you want?" says Tyler.

Bradley opens up to him.

"Tyler, I know we have our differences, but I just wanted to let you know that I hope this doesn't mean anything. I just wanted to go back to the good old days as friends."

"Really? After everything I did to you, you'd forgive me? What game are you playing?" Tyler says with a sniffle.

"This isn't a trick. I just want you to change for the better," Bradley says with a serious face. He sticks out his hand. "Let's start over. Friends?"

Feeling guilty, Tyler pauses for a moment. Then he hugs Bradley, and he starts sobbing.

"I'm sorry I did all this to you. I just wanted to be cool ... Honest. I'm sorry, Junior, for doubting you. I promise I'll change." Bradley smiles and hugs him back, also crying.

Later that afternoon, the whole village gathers around the yard. People whisper to each other about what a tree can do. Especially for two people in particular, who were once friends. Now united once again, enjoying wonderful pie until the sun sets. For years to come, the people of the village would know how much happiness a tree can bring.

Masked Emotions

by Eirini Katsika

Noah was at the mask store.

He had a date tonight with a girl from work. Her name was Sophia. She liked sports, hiking, and working out. So, Noah had to make sure he got a mask that would make him appear adventurous and athletic. It didn't matter that he didn't like sports, and even the thought of going on long walks bored him. What mattered was that Sophia liked them.

He just hoped she hadn't seen him at work because there he wore a different mask. That mask said that he enjoyed his work, even though he hated it. That he loved his coworkers, even though they were fake, backstabbing snakes. That he was confident, although he was scared to talk to anyone, to the point that he couldn't wait to go back to his apartment and take that mask off. To finally be himself, even for a little bit.

"Oh, this is one of our most popular masks," the saleswoman said to Noah, hiding behind her own mask. "You simply must try it. I am telling you; you are going to love it." And she shoved him into one of the changing rooms.

Noah took his mask off. He breathed in deeply. It felt good, so good that for a second, he thought of going out there without it. Like himself. For the whole world to see who he really was. Was he really that bad that he had to hide it? He enjoyed being alone. That must mean something. It meant that he was a loner, and a loser, and no one was going to like him.

Noah tried on the new mask. Just like the rest, it felt foreign, like it wasn't a part of him. It fit his face, and yet it felt too small or too big. He wasn't sure. It made his face feel itchy and he wanted to rip it off. Yet, he bought it anyway and thanked the saleswoman for pushing him to buy it.

Noah got out of the store. There were people everywhere protesting and to his surprise, none of them wore a mask. Something in his chest tightened. They looked angry. Yet, it wasn't the reason why he felt so uncomfortable. They showed their real emotions, their true, bare selves. And they looked proud about it.

They were brave, and that unsettled him.

A group of them was holding a banner that said: "Show your face. Show who you truly are. You are beautiful."

Did they really believe that? Every passer-by, including himself, was looking at them like they were crazy.

For a quick second, he thought of joining them. What would happen if he took his mask off and became one of the brave protestors?

Noah panicked.

He had to go.

He was going to be late for his date. He couldn't be late. He was never late. He tried to push through the crowd, but it was hard. There were so many people, and they kept chanting, "Burn the masks. Burn all the masks." With each passing minute, they were getting angrier.

Noah finally managed to slip through them.

What if...?

A question tried to make its way through Noah's mind, but he hastily shoved it away.

He would have to take the long road to the restaurant, but if he ran, he might make it there in time or a minute or two late.

Noah ran down the road and turned right. As he passed in front of a school, he stopped. None of the kids were wearing masks. They looked happy. There was a group of kids playing ball. Others were reading. A different group was walking around, talking. They all had their own group where they belonged. A group that accepted them for who they were because they had the same interests.

But Noah knew not all kids felt like that. Not everyone felt like they belonged. Was that when his mask went on? Noah wondered.

Noah took the way to the restaurant again. Only this time he didn't run. Didn't even think that he was going to be late. What did it matter if he was late anyway? It wouldn't change anything.

Noah finally made it to the restaurant. He walked in and followed the waitress to the table. Sophia was already there, waiting for him. She smiled. Noah couldn't be sure if it was a genuine smile or if she was hiding a different feeling under that mask.

They ordered, and then talked about how she travelled around Europe while Noah thought of how much he hated flying. Dreaded it to be exact. The only way his mother got him to get on a plane was by sedating him. Sophia talked about her pets. She had two dogs, but Noah couldn't remember their names. He was more of a cat person himself. He had a cat named Vito, the only creature that had seen him without the mask. The first day Noah took it off in front of him, the cat simply started rubbing himself on his leg and purring. Didn't get scared. Didn't run away.

He wondered if he took off his mask right now, what would Sophia's reaction be? Get up and leave, and pretend she didn't know him? Get up and leave screaming? Or would she stay?

Noah got up; Sophia pretended she wasn't surprised by his sudden move. He was going to do it. He was going to take that mask off and to hell with everything.

"What are you doing?" Sophia asked, looking around to see if people were staring at them, but kept that fake smile on.

Noah's palms started to sweat. His throat felt clogged up and burning. No words could come out, and his head started to spin.

"I am sorry," he stuttered and took a step back almost knocking the chair down. He caught it fast. "I need to go to the bathroom." His voice sounded strange, rough even to his own ears.

He took a few steps, but suddenly everything was spinning, and he couldn't see clearly. He hit something or someone, and his mask slipped from his face and fell to the ground.

"I am sorry. I am so, so sorry," Noah apologized.

"Are you alright?" A beautiful female voice asked him. She sounded genuine.

"I..." Noah looked down and saw his mask lying there on the ground. Thin needles pierced his skin from his fingertips all the way up to his arms. His heart was beating fast. He was standing there, in front of all these people, without wearing his mask. Completely naked.

"Noah?"

Something in her voice, how his name came out of her lips coated with concern, forced him to take his eyes away from the mask and to her captivating face. That olive skin, and big, brown eyes. There was kindness on that bare face. No mask, just her. She looked serene; at peace with herself.

It was then that Noah realized he knew her. It was Eva from school. The only person who stood by him when those guys bullied him. Before he decided to put on the mask and join them instead. But she stayed the same. Of course, she did.

"How are you?" Eva asked him.

When was the last time anyone asked him that? Or the last time anyone cared to know how he truly was? He hadn't even thought of his true emotions in so long that he didn't even know how to answer.

Noah looked at his table. Sophia was staring at him like he was something ugly. So did everybody else in the restaurant, pinning him with their eyes full of disgust. Everyone except Eva, who was standing there like all those people gawking at them and judging them didn't affect her. He also noticed she was wearing a golden necklace of a little cat.

He could put the mask back on and be invisible again, be like everybody else, and hide how he truly felt. But he had lost so much time hiding behind that mask. He had lost his true self.

"Do you like cats?" Noah asked instead.

"I actually have two. How about you?"

Noah smiled. A true smile. It felt good. It felt normal. Like being reborn.

Flame

The worst loneliness is to not be comfortable with yourself.
— Mark Twain

A Day in the Life of a Horrible Jerk

by H. Issaq

When the first rays of sunlight spilled through the window of his home, Bog sat up in his bed and stretched his arms overhead with an exaggerated yawn. Of course, calling a hole in the hollowed-out tree he lived in a window is generous, and calling a pile of dead leaves a bed is even more so. He stood up and vigorously shook his entire body to rid himself of any leaves that might have gotten into his hair and pajamas. He stumbled over to his food cache and helped himself to some of the mushrooms he'd gathered the day before. He'd been incredibly lucky to find them; he had spotted a rabbit eating them, so he beat him up and took every last one. It might have been a cruel and selfish thing to do, but Bog was a cruel and selfish guy. A cruel and selfish guy with all the mushrooms he could want.

His belly full, he shed his pajamas and walked out of his house with purpose. He didn't slow down as he approached the nearby pond, taking a deep breath in before walking straight into the water. Once the water was over his head, he walked around in circles a few times and quickly scrubbed his armpits before walking back out. He kept walking until he was back at his tree, heading inside to get dressed for work.

Bog had a very important job. He was the local trickster, terrorizing the humans in the nearby village with pranks and petty crimes. He was self-appointed, of course; no other fae lived in the area, and the other inhabitants of the forest hated him passionately. When he wasn't tying the human's shoelaces together or replacing the freshly laid eggs in the chicken coops with rotten ones, he would share his mischief with his neighbors. There wasn't any particular reason for it, apart from his general love of chaos and enjoyment of the misery of others. The neighbors had exhausted every option to protect themselves from Bog's torment, from asking nicely to traps and security systems. After realizing that there was no way to stop him, all they could do was curse and yell at him if they saw him approaching their homes.

After a long day of putting holes in the roofs of every building in the village, Bog decided to turn in. On his way home he crossed paths with Mrs. Hedgehog. The old woman was power-walking by on her hind legs, pumping her arms for extra speed. She was carrying a rather full-looking bag on her shoulder.

"Where ya going, you old bat?" Bog sneered.

"Go to hell, Bog!" Mrs. Hedgehog called back, never breaking her stride. Bog scoffed.

"I'm already in hell! I live next to *you*, and you stink! You walk around with turds caught in your quills!" Mrs. Hedgehog responded by flipping Bog off over her shoulder as she continued on her way.

"That lady, I swear..." Bog grumbled. He wondered again where the old woman was heading and decided to follow her. Maybe he would come up with a fun way to spoil her evening.

Despite their unpleasant interaction, Mrs. Hedgehog appeared to be in very high spirits. Bog struggled to keep up with her without making too much noise. She slipped between the trees, crossed a log bridge over a stream, and scampered up a hill. As Bog trailed behind her, he couldn't help but feel as though he'd never been in that area of the forest before. The air felt tingly and heavy, and he felt like he could taste something earthy on the breeze. As he trudged up the hill, the ground felt... fluffy? It felt like he was walking on fresh loaves of bread, the ground squishing down and back up again with each step.

"What the hell is going on here?" Bog muttered, feeling uncharacteristically anxious in such strange conditions (although he would never admit that, because what, is he some kind of baby?). Suddenly remembering why he was there in the first place, he looked around for Mrs. Hedgehog. He spotted her just as she had reached the top of the hill, disappearing over the edge.

Uncertain of his footing on the spongy terrain, Bog climbed the rest of the way up on his hands and knees. At the top, he settled down onto his stomach and peered over the edge. The hilltop was a beautiful sight; a wide-open space peppered with flowers and berry bushes, and a great big apple tree under which Mrs. Hedgehog was setting up a picnic. Bathed in the golden light of the setting sun, the scene was enchanting enough to bring tears to Bog's eyes. He gasped.

"Crying is for nerds and babies!" he exclaimed, furiously wiping his eyes. He sighed with relief when his vision cleared. "Phew! Good thing nobody saw that."

"Oh, for the love of—why can't you let anyone enjoy anything?!" Bog looked around for the source of the complaint only to see Mrs. Hedgehog glowering at him with a blueberry in hand. Her eyes seemed comically large, sparkling with all the colors of the rainbow. "Let me start my day in peace, you bipedal rat!"

"You're one to talk! And what the hell is going on with your face?! Your eyes are almost the size of that friggin' blueberry you're holding!" As soon as he finished speaking, Bog's environment began to shift. He could hear Mrs. Hedgehog's voice but couldn't quite make out what she was saying. All he could focus on were the colors and shapes moving around him, the whole world swirling and glowing and humming. He struggled to his feet only to lose his footing and roll down the hill, bouncing off the trees and landing flat on his back at the bottom. He peered up through the fluttering leaves of the treetops at the watery sky, orange spilling into pinks and purples as the sun continued to set.

As he struggled to understand the situation, Bog began to visualize the events of the previous day. He could see himself wailing on that rabbit, *really* clobbering him, before collecting all the mushrooms and running away laughing. His vision melted into a scene of that morning, when he was gorging on mushrooms and joyfully reminiscing about his violent means of acquiring them. He felt... kind of bad about it. A little nauseous, too. He had never experienced anything like shame or guilt before, but he assumed that those were the feelings responsible for the thick coating of slime he suddenly felt on all his internal organs. Maybe he could have left the rabbit with, like, *one* mushroom. And maybe he could have done without those last few kicks and punches.

Bog sighed and stood up once again, his legs tingling and gelatinous as he wobbled his way home. He moved very slowly; the sun had completely set by the time he made it to the log. Mrs. Hedgehog passed him on her way back.

"You're always annoying, but you're being even more of a weirdo than usual. Get outta my way, you blockhead." She shoved him aside and scuttled over the log bridge. Bog continued his slow journey home, dragging a small branch along the tree trunks as he passed them. This resulted in the most beautiful noise, shimmering sound waves rippling out with each tap. Bog eventually found himself before the pond he bathed in every day and was lost in the image of the moon reflected on its surface. As the white circle wriggled and danced on the water, he heard the voice of the moon itself speaking to him.

*You're a **big** jerk. And you shouldn't have eaten those mushrooms. What are you, stupid?*

At that moment, Bog had an epiphany: he was having some sort of mental breakdown. It was the only explanation. Mrs. Hedgehog's gigantic eyeballs, the general silliness of his environment, *emotions*. He must have been losing his mind! And maybe... maybe it was because he was *finally* seeing the error of his ways! Maybe he *shouldn't* harm and inconvenience others for fun. Maybe he should try to be kind and loving to everyone around him. It all made perfect sense.

"Duh. I'm so friggin' smart," Bog muttered smugly. With his realizations settling deep into his chest with a feeling of intense warmth, Bog floated back home and collapsed into his bed. He fell asleep in seconds.

The following day, Bog was so physically and emotionally exhausted that he could barely move. He managed to crawl his way to the pond to wash up, and on his way back he found Ms. Squirrel and her children having some snacks and drinking some apple juice. Bog was initially inspired to rob them, but he remembered his experience from the day before. He approached the family and cleared his throat.

"Hi—"

"Holy shit! Kids, stay back," the mother yelped, immediately placing herself between Bog and her children. "We don't want any trouble, Bog. Leave us alone."

"Could you just... I just wanted to ask if I could have some juice," Bog said. He held up his hands. "See? No weapons or nothin'. Just using my words and asking nicely."

"Oh." Ms. Squirrel looked around as though she was expecting something else to happen. "Are you... you're serious?" Bog nodded, gritting his teeth to stop himself from calling her names. "Well, all right then! We can spare some juice, I guess." Ms. Squirrel poured some juice from a large acorn pitcher into a small cup and handed it to Bog, who immediately chugged it. He handed the cup back to Ms. Squirrel, who was looking at him as though she was expecting something from him.

"Uh... th-thank you?" The words felt awkward coming out of his mouth, but Ms. Squirrel appeared delighted to hear them.

"Anytime, neighbor! And thank *you* for asking instead of robbing us!" Ms. Squirrel laughed and playfully smacked Bog on the shoulder, and it made him want to lie down and die. "I'm so glad you've finally changed your ways! Now we can all be one big happy community."

Bog mumbled something about needing to release all the livestock in the human village and quickly walked away. One big happy community? That sounded about as fun as eating shards of glass. Not to mention all the vomiting he would inevitably be doing if he kept up with all that please-and-thank-you crap. Hard pass.

The following day, Bog went back to his usual shitty antics.

The Forest Fire

by Comet C.

It was mid-fall when it happened.

The sun had just set over their small cabin in the woods where Klar was preparing the house for the harsh winter that lay ahead. His task was to check and clean the fireplace before his boyfriend returned with chopped wood.

Klar thought his lover would have been back sooner, considering the walk had been short enough. He brushed off his concerns as his anxiety trying to get the best of him. He knew that the forest was safe, but he could not shake off the uneasiness as he moved to check the fireplace.

As he stretched to clean a smudge off the fireplace mirror, Klar sharply gasped at what he saw in the reflection. What he saw was no smudge.

He spun to face the window. What he saw made him feel weak. Outside was a black plume of smoke, growing above the treeline. A forest fire had started right where Klar had sent his boyfriend.

Klar tore through the house for the fire extinguisher and med kit. He did not care for the mess he made in the process and barely put on his boots before rushing outside.

On the verge of a panic attack, Klar sped towards the source of the smoke, stumbling several times over rocks, tree roots, and his untied laces. He realized he was out of shape but continued to run, even as his whole body begged him to stop.

"Please be okay," Klar begged as he pushed himself to run faster. "Please be okay..."

He kept going, even as he reached the start of the smoke. He knew of his weak lung condition and how the smoke could suffocate him. He would not turn back until he found his boyfriend.

Covering his mouth with the sleeve of his sweater, Klar continued running.

He only stopped when he could no longer see, and his gasps for air became wheezing coughs.

"Theo?!" Klar called out into the smoke. "Where are you?!" he coughed.

Squinting through the smoke, Klar saw a strange figure a few feet in front of him. The figure was humanoid yet wasn't. It was several inches taller than Klar. It had two pairs of tall, jagged horns sprouting from its head and large bat-like wings spread behind it.

Klar staggered backward in fear but tripped on his laces. He fell hard on his back, knocking out the air from his lungs. He gasped for air, but the thick smoke began to suffocate him.

Klar watched in terror as the figure lunged toward him.

"Theo...!" he wheezed as he lost consciousness.

Klar awoke in the town's hospital with a breathing mask secured tightly to his face.

He blinked, confused on how he got there. He quickly remembered his endangered boyfriend and frantically pulled at the breathing mask.

He was stopped by a hand calmly pressing on his chest.

Klar turned to see Theo sitting in the chair by the bed.

"You're safe now, breathe." Theo spoke softly, kissing Klar on the forehead.

The sight of his boyfriend was enough to make Klar cry. "What happened?" he breathed heavily through the mask. "The fire..."

"I dealt with it," Theo interrupted. "You shouldn't have gone to the fire. If I didn't reach you in time..." He paused, turning away slightly.

"I just wanted to make sure you were okay..." Klar sniffled.

Theo turned to look Klar in the eyes. "I'm... okay." He sighed softly.

Klar's mind flashed back to what he saw before he fainted. "I saw something in the woods... a *monster*."

"Monster?!" Theo raised his voice as he quickly stood up from the chair. His anger quickly changed to shock. He backed away slightly, stumbling over the chair.

Klar froze. He was surprised but not afraid of his lover's sudden burst of anger. "What-what are you saying?"

"Please don't freak out..." Theo replied anxiously. He refused to make eye contact with Klar. "There's been something I wanted to tell you for a while... but wasn't sure how you'd react..."

Theo was shaking.

Klar slowly sat up from the hospital bed, removing the breathing mask to see Theo better. "Why would I think differently of you?" He grew concerned.

"You said I was a *monster*." Theo frowned, and Klar could tell there was sadness behind his eyes.

Klar regretted his choice of words. He sighed. "Sit with me."

Theo hesitated but sat on the bed. He flinched even as Klar carefully embraced him.

"I'm sorry I said that." Klar spoke softly. "I had no idea that was you back there. I don't think you're a monster and I never will. I love you so much." He kissed Theo's shoulder before resting on him.

"I-I love you too," Theo replied, looking down at his feet. Klar felt Theo's mind was elsewhere.

The two sat in silence. Klar was unsure what to think of the situation. He had millions of questions. "Could I ask you something?" he started, hoping to get an answer to at least one of his questions.

Theo took a deep breath. "Sure, go ahead..." He anxiously grabbed at the collar of his shirt.

Klar pondered for a moment. He had to be sure his question wouldn't hurt his lover's feelings again. "What's it like?"

Theo stared up at the ceiling as he took a deep breath in.

"Sorry..." Klar quickly added. "You don't have to answer any questions if it makes you feel uneasy."

"No..." Theo responded immediately. "I'm ready." He took another deep breath before turning his head towards Klar. "I should probably start by explaining the fire. I caused it, I'm sorry, I didn't mean for it to get so bad..."

Klar looked at Theo with wide eyes. "*You* started the fire? How? All you brought with you was that... axe..." He stopped talking as he realized. "Are you...?"

"Part dragon..." Theo finished the sentence hesitantly. "Please don't freak out, I know it's strange..." He looked at the ground again.

"No! Not at all!" Klar perked up excitedly. "That's really cool! Can you breathe fire? Is that what caused the forest fire?" Klar could tell he was overloading Theo with questions. He sat back patiently for his response.

Theo jerked his head up and blinked in shock. It was as if he expected a different reaction. "I *can* breathe fire, but it's awkward. Although, I can also launch fire from my hands." He moved a hand away from Klar to bring flames to his fingertips. "I tried to cut a tree down with fire... and well... you know how that went..." He laughed sheepishly.

Klar watched the spectacle with starry eyes. "That's so cool! Why would you ever hide this?"

Theo looked somberly at his feet, making Klar regret his words again.

"I'm sorry..." Klar apologized again. "That was a dumb question, wasn't it?"

"No, not at all." Theo kissed Klar softly on the cheek. "It's just not extremely easy for me... but I'm glad you aren't afraid of me, knowing what I am."

Klar looked up at Theo in concern. "Have... have you told anyone this before?"

Sadness stretched over Theo's face. "Yeah... and let's say that didn't go so well either..." He looked back down. "I've decided to keep it a secret since then... so I wouldn't lose anyone else..." He shook his head in shame.

Klar embraced Theo tightly. "I'm so sorry... I'm glad you told me though. I love you all the same." He smiled up at him.

Theo's mood improved, and he smiled back. "I love you too! Have any more questions for me?" he chuckled, seeming relieved.

"Millions! But I won't overload you with all of them right now." Klar giggled. "Wait, can you *fly*? You had wings back there!"

Theo laughed, looking away bashfully. "Yeah." He continued smiling. "I could show you if you'd like?"

"Yes! I'd love to!" His smile faded as he remembered his condition. "But, what about..." He gestured to the breathing mask next to him.

"Don't worry." Theo smirked. "You only had a couple bruises from the fall. I spoke to the doctor earlier and they said we'd be good to go as soon as you woke up." He got up from the bed and moved to open the single large window.

Klar giggled as Theo took him in his arms and stepped towards the open window. He watched in awe as Theo summoned his wings and stretched them far behind him, almost stretching to the other side of the small room.

"You ready?" Theo smiled.

"Always." Klar beamed back, holding on tight as they took off into the night.

Simulated Minds

by Ailsa Allan

Clarke wakes with a jerk. She finds herself lying on a bed and dressed in nothing but a hospital gown. Slightly panicking, Clarke takes in her surroundings. The room is perfectly square and coated in white. A round mirror hangs to her right, and on her left is a metal shelf devoid of objects except for a tiny gargoyle statue. On the far wall, a single door stands. She pushes herself from the bed and scrambles for the door. Clarke reaches for the nob, only to find it locked.

"Clarke, I need you to stay calm, okay?"

She jumps at the voice, and her eyes frantically search the room. "Who's there?"

"It's the little gargoyle statue."

Clarke's eyes shoot toward the small shelf and lock on the tiny figure. Her heart hammers in her chest as she stares it down, waiting for the object to move. The gargoyle stays stock-still.

"This has to be some fucked up dream," Clarke mutters.

"It's not a dream, Clarke," the gargoyle replies, causing the woman to yelp and fall backwards onto the bed. "This is all part of the trials. It's a simulation."

"No! That doesn't make any sense! I was just—" The words die in her throat, and Clarke realizes in horror that she can't remember. Who was she before she woke up?

"Clarke," the gargoyle starts again, "I know this all seems confusing, but you will understand soon enough."

Bewildered and frightened, Clarke shoots out a finger at the small statue. "No, don't say a word! You're not supposed to say anything!" She stands from the bed and paces the floor, racking her brain for any memory of how she got here. She comes up short and cries, "Why can't I remember anything?!"

"Clarke, listen to me!" the statue exclaims. "You were drugged."

"*Drugged?!*" Clarke shouts, her thoughts going a mile a minute. "By *whom*?"

"I cannot tell you that information. It is against the trial's policy."

"Bullshit!" Clarke swings a fist into the mirror. Glass shatters, and her knuckles come away bloody. She stares at her hand, and a smile pulls at her lips.

"I need you to listen to me, Clarke," the gargoyle continues as Clarke slides to the floor. "This drug will mess with your sanity, but you can't let it win, or you will fail."

Clarke picks up a shard of glass and studies herself in the reflection. Her eyes are bloodshot, and the pupils are blown wide. The sight makes her giggle.

"The drug takes you through four stages: temporary memory loss, an uncontrollable episode of laughter, hysterical crying, and then a depressing numbness. If you make it through the stages, you move on."

Clarke ignores the figure. "You're lying!" she giggles, but it soon turns into laughter. "A liar!" Tears glide down her cheeks as the laugh turns manic. Clarke wipes at her wet eyes, her stomach clenching with the power of her laughter. She finally looks at the gargoyle and states, "You must think I'm crazy."

"No, Clarke," the gargoyle replies, "I don't think you're crazy; that's the drug talking."

Her laughter suddenly stops, but her tears continue to fall. "But I *am* crazy. I should be strapped to the bed—*that's* how crazy I am." She sniffs as more tears stream down her cheeks. A loud sob rips through the room. "I mean, look at me! I'm talking to a gargoyle statue, for fuck's sake!" Her chest heaves with cries, and snot drips from her nose while she hyperventilates. Clarke rocks back and forth until her tears slow, and hiccups interrupt her inhales. Small whines sound in her throat as she sluggishly wipes her eyes.

Her mind becomes a haze, and her eyes unfocus. Her back rests against the wall as her limbs go slack. A numbness spreads across her body as she sits there, and Clarke tunes into the ringing of her ears in the silent room.

Time passes—for two minutes or two hours? Clarke doesn't know. She slowly comes to her senses and scans her surroundings. She finds the gargoyle still perched on the shelf and the shattered mirror on the ground. Raising her injured hand, Clarke notices the flakes of dry blood on her knuckles. Finally, she clears her throat and croaks, "I remember."

"That's good, Clarke," the statue voices. "What do you remember?"

"All of it," she whispers. "The doctors, the tools, the other subjects... It could've been anyone else, so why me? Why did they choose me?"

"I understand you're confused, Clarke, but there's nothing to worry about."

The woman stays quiet and focuses her attention on her hand again. "You know," she prompts, "the doctors told me this trial is supposed to '*prove*' something." She looks at the door and gives a light scoff. "I think they just wanted an excuse to drug a bunch of people and watch them go insane." Her head lolls to the side, her eyes landing on the gargoyle. "But that's unethical, isn't it."

The gargoyle only stares back, unmoving.

Clarke moves to a stand and approaches the statue. She tilts her head as she peers closer. "You're one of them, aren't you?"

The figure stays silent for a beat before saying, "Clarke, don't do anything reckless." The woman furrows her brows at the monotone voice. She opens her mouth to respond, but the gargoyle continues. "It's all part of the simulation. You have to under—"

Clarke hurls the figure at the wall, breaking it, and pieces scatter the floor. Alarms blare from the other side of the door.

"Fuck you and your simulations!" she yells. "I am done!"

Heavy pounding on the door follows, and Clarke jumps into action. She hurries over to the broken mirror and grabs a large piece of glass before crouching behind the side of the bed and watching the door. The pounding continues until the door suddenly bursts open, and Clarke freezes. There in the doorway stands a replica of herself, breathing heavily.

"We need to go now!" Clarke 2.0 exclaims, rushing into the room.

Clarke jumps up and points the shard in defence. "Who are you?!"

"They call me Lara. I'm your simulation twin!"

Clarke raises a brow. "So, you're with the doctors?"

Lara hesitates. "Not exactly. The doctors *created* me for the simulation."

"What—"

"I know that sounds confusing, but we don't have time to discuss this!" Lara takes a step forward. "Do you hear those sirens? They've released their abominations that will be here any second! We need to move!"

Clarke glares at her simulation twin, not making any effort to move. "How do I know I can trust you?"

Lara groans in frustration. "We don't have time for this! Just put down the glass!"

"Fine, but I swear if this is some sort of trick, I will kill you," Clarke responds, tossing the piece of glass to the side.

"Yeah, I know," Lara mutters, grabbing Clarke's arm. "Now, let's go!"

They move out of the room, and the alarm pierces their ears. Overhead, the lights flash red. Similar to the room, the hallway is painted white, like a psych ward. Clarke chuckles bitterly at the sight.

"Stay close and follow me!" Lara yells over the alarm. They jog to the end of the hall, passing more doors.

"What's behind those doors?" Clarke questions.

"More simulation rooms," Lara pants and glances around the corner before adding, "and trial subjects." She motions forward, and they head down another hallway.

"But why? Why are there so many?"

Lara suddenly stops and turns to face Clarke, her face tense. "Doctors call it the 'Simulation Twin Trials.' They send hundreds of subjects into this simulation to challenge their subconscious. The subject's simulation twin—which, in your case, is me—has an hour to find our psyche twin and break them out. If we fail, we both die." She glances at her wrist, and Clarke notices the watch she wears.

"How do you know all this?"

Lara smirks. "Like I said, I'm part of this simulation. The doctors created me for the trial."

Clarke blinks in disbelief. "So, you only exist because I was sent here?"

"Bingo." Lara's smirk widens a smidge before dropping as her eyes catch sight of movement behind Clarke. She loudly swears. "Time to go!"

Clarke whips around and shouts, "What the fuck are those?" Four human-like creatures hobble up the hallway, growling and screeching. Their skin is ash grey, and mutated limbs stick out on their bony bodies.

Lara grabs Clarke's arm and hurriedly pulls her along. "Those are the Forgotten Twins," she explains. "They were the first creations of the simulation, but the doctors abandoned them because they didn't turn out right." Clarke risks a glance back, and Lara adds, "Now, with the trials, the doctors use them to their advantage. Sick bastards."

They continue down the hall at a light jog, passing more rooms.

"Where are we even going?" Clarke exclaims, slightly out of breath as a stitch in her side begins to form.

Lara stops at the end of the hall and glances around the corner. "It's called the Mirror Mind. It's a giant portal that allows your psyche to travel from the simulation world to the real world." She motions to continue, and they turn down another hallway. "If I remember correctly, we should be close." Lara takes another glance at her watch. "Five minutes."

With their chests heaving, Clarke and Lara finally round the last corner, and at last, the Mirror Mind stands alone in the open area. The seven-foot reflective glass shimmers silver like molten lead. Its edges are bordered in dark titanium.

"Holy shit."

Lara sighs in relief. "Beautiful, isn't it."

"Yeah," Clarke says in awe and steps closer to the portal. "It's incredible."

A loud beep breaks her out of the trance, and she looks at Lara, who grimly stares back. "60 seconds."

With a terse nod, Clarke reaches out to her simulation twin. "We do this together." Lara takes her hand, and they move forward. About a foot from the entrance, Clarke abruptly halts, exclaiming, "Wait!"

Lara frowns. "Clarke, we need to—"

"What will happen to you?"

The question throws Lara off guard, and she shrugs. "I guess we'll find out." She squeezes Clarke's hand in reassurance and smiles. "Ready?" The latter nods, and with a few seconds left, they walk into the Mirror Mind.

"Welcome back, Clarke."

The Angry Trick or Treater

by Zoe Farmer

October 30th, 2018

I rose from the grey, creaking bunk bed to hear the phone buzzing from the old, white, wooden desk. I turned off the alarm and walked over to my broken door. I put my fragile ears against it to hear the extremely aggressive sounds of people arguing. I soon came to realize it was my parents. They always argue. They never do anything but argue.

I opened the door and peeked out to see my parents. My mother was making a salad, and my dad was sitting on one of the dining room chairs. She quickly noticed I was standing behind the door. Mother decided to shout "Hey Hunny" at me, but I walked by them without speaking a single word. I marched into the marble kitchen and got to work eating my yellow pancakes which were stacked beautifully on my plate.

My parents started approaching the white, expensive kitchen acting like everything was fine. So, I decided to take the plate of juicy food to my room instead to avoid confrontation. I crept by them, and just went into my room, closing the door behind me.

Once I got on my bed, I felt a feeling I'd never felt before. My head started to get dizzy like I was upside down in a bad roller coaster. My stomach felt queasy and unwell. I started to panic, and I felt my body start to shake. Then, my small body crashed to the firm surface below me. A white, foamy liquid started bubbling and dropping from my wet, pink lips. I felt scared and alone. I couldn't hear anything since my ears were numb. I thought I was about to perish by myself until a heard a crash from my door being knocked down by my mother and father. They both bent to the floor, my father putting my head on my mother's knees. The rest of the night became a blur.

October 31st, 2018

Then, my hazel eyes slowly started to crack open. My body was weak like I was drugged with some hard medication. A sore throat caught my attention, as it was hard to swallow the cup of water that was on the stand beside the white hospital bed. I felt weak and worthless. I turned to see Mom looking at me with a relieved smile. Water dripped out of her eyes and started falling down her small, narrow face. She tried covering it up with a cackling laugh. But we both knew she was full of fear from what had happened.

We talked for a few moments before my mother forced my body upwards, and Dad strolled through the door to see me lying in the bed. He held a green outfit in his hand. I realized Halloween had approached without me even noticing.

The costume had a green headband, with an object poking out the top shaped like an eyeball. My mother gestured for me to try it on. I went to the bathroom to shimmy myself into the outfit and I realized it was an alien. I loved aliens because of the news reports of the "Area 51" sightings. I watched the reports every single day to see if we had new life coming to our planet. After I excitedly threw on the costume, my mother put on a white plastic coat that looked like it was made of bubble wrap. My father did the same and pointed towards the door, and we as a family walked out of the building.

We then made our way around the neighbourhood retrieving candy from our community like Tootsies, Aeros, and way more. After we spent hours walking around the busy streets, we noticed one more house was left. The three of us slowly strolled towards the home. It looked like it was made in the 1960s, but not one piece of the paint was chipped. The house had a bunch of creepy decorations like zombies and ghosts. The man who owned the house had thinning, grey hair and was sitting cross legged on his white bench decorated with spiders.

We went towards the black paved driveway. We approached the man. He just started laughing, pointing, and making fun of the costume I was wearing. The costume was too "cheap" and "disgusting".

"I refuse to give candy to horrible costumes. You look stupid but you can try again next year." Tears started falling down my face until the couple forced me away from the old man.

***

30 minutes after we had already gotten home from the journey around the neighbourhood, I felt a feeling of execution. My anger got to me. I had had a rough day and he made it even worse by making me feel worthless. I was going to show him who he had messed with.

I started to feel a rush of adrenaline as I broke out of the white window of the room, I was staying in. I ran to the front of the yard and turned around to see if I had woken anyone in the household up. I started aggressively pacing back and forth across the green, wet grass, trying to wrap my pink and mushy brain around the idea I was having at that given moment.

I heard a creepy voice that sounded like it would be in a horror movie. The voice started chattering at me repeatedly and it got more aggressive each time. I could not tolerate it anymore and I let the voice take over me as I pulled my hair in multiple different directions. It kept taunting me as I was losing my mind. Then the voice stopped and all and all I saw was pictures of murder. I never thought I would commit a crime, but my brain felt that was being forced to.

I started pacing even harder trying to get the image out of my head. Teeth chattering. Hair pulling. Nail biting. This was all happening during a time of fear and anger. I felt devotion to my brain. I felt like a puppet and my brain was controlling the strings. My body was stiff, and I could not stop moving; I had no control over anything.

I crept up to the old man's home that fueled my burning rage. The devil took over and my demons came out to play. I looked at the house and a devilish grin appeared on my narrow face.

I decided to finish what I came here to do. I walked up the stairs to pick the old lock. After a few minutes, the door was finally freed from the chains. I walked in and crept up the old creaking stairs that faced the door. I quickly noticed there was only one door that was closed, which was a little bit suspicious. He was making this too easy for me. I quickly opened the door to find a massive king-sized bed that had red satin sheets with black leather pillows. I looked around to find the creepy old man sleeping peacefully. I saw a pillow that stood out from the others. The pillow had blue birds flying on the exterior. I peeked over at the man with a smile that could boil your skin.

I walked close to his hollow ear, and I whispered softly, "you messed with the wrong person," as I slammed the pillow down on his face. The pillow blocked out all his heatless screams. The old man tried crying for help, but his lungs were slowly collapsing. His airways started closing until there was no noise to be heard throughout the room. His arms collapsed and the heart that was rapidly beating had finally stopped.

I removed the pillow to see his cold, dead face lying there. I just stood there, seeing what I had done to the grumpy man. I felt sadness, then a wave of regret. I felt a rush of panic. My brain started realizing I had to cover it up quick or I was going to be in a lot of trouble. I rolled the body off the bed, down the stairs and into the kitchen where I started chopping up the body while crying a river of tears. First went the legs, then the arms, next was the femur and the heart was near the end. His brain was tiny but that was the last piece that needed chopping.

I went into his garage and grabbed a bottle of chlorine. I kept soaking his body in the liquid until his skeleton started to dry and slowly dissolve. It was then time for the dirty job.

I ripped out a big piece of the carpet flooring and all that was underneath was dirt. I grabbed a shovel and started digging until I had a hole big enough to put a body in. I rolled the body into the hole and covered it back up with the piles of dirt. I put the carpet back, as if nothing had been moved or touched. I bathed the carpet with bleach until there was no traces of blood left. The carpet looked as if it had gotten a new shine.

Little did I know, the police officers were called by the neighbours who had heard a bunch of rumbling in the house. A few seconds later, I heard knocks on the door. My chest felt like it was about to have a heart attack. I opened the door with a big bright smile on my face.

The police said, "Hey kid, is everything alright here?"

I just nodded and invited the kind officers in for some cookies and tea to shy away from what I had done seconds before they had arrived.

The police spent a few minutes there and I acted like the old man was my uncle that I was house sitting for the old man because he went on vacation. Then, the police realized everything was fine, so they got up to leave.

I burst into tears. It just happened and I could not control it. The police officer ran over to me with panic. All I could do was point towards the floor tiles where the man was buried.

All I could say was, "He is right there."

Pup

by C.Kaneway

These days, the forest looks less and less scary, and less and less dark. I can still remember, though those memories are getting vague and foggy now, how the trees and the shadows looked when we last sang. Back then, I stayed in the den and played with my brothers and sisters while all the parents went out to hunt. I was afraid of the woods then, so I didn't even want to come along.

Today, though, I'm old enough to tag along. The forest isn't so scary anymore. Maybe I'm putting on a brave face for my siblings here with me; not all of them look as confident as I feel. Maybe it's for the sake of the parents guiding us; these are **my** parents after all. Still, I'm taking charge of this group of pups and marching right behind my mother.

She's called *She-with-the-best-nose*. She is small for a mother, with a coat like old snow with irregular streaks of the night sky. Her eyes are like tree bark or fallen leaves, but with light behind them. There's no wind, so her nose is close to the ground right now because she's trying to find the colour of walking meat. Every wolf has a nose that can pick up that colour, but hers can follow it further than anyone else in the family.

I imitate her and agitate my nostrils to find the right colour, but I quickly get distracted by the other pups running around. Father calls to us to stop being a nuisance, but that only gets me thinking about him.

He's called *He-who-pays-most-attention*; his coat is like bare summer dirt, but the fur around his nose and the tip of his tail are like fresh snow. His eyes have a lot of light in them, but they almost never look at us pups, or at mother. They look this way and that, both around us and far away. His ears turn about even more, and never to where he's looking. He isn't big either, but he's bigger than mother. Unlike her, he's old. Old enough to take his meal right after *He-who-guides-all*, the leader of our family, and *He-who-knows-best*, the eldest of the family.

All this thinking of names makes me think it's time I have a name too! When a mother or a father want my attention from far away, they just call me *Pup*. They call every pup that. When I'm not paying attention or if I'm being stupid, they call me *Pup-who-knows-nothing*. They call every pup that too, when they deserve it. And I don't want to end up with a stupid name like *He-who-walks-slow*. That name is probably why he gets his meal after everyone else. So, I need to come up with my own name; I think.

What about... *He-who-is-most-brave*? That's certainly how I feel right now, so I sound it out. *She-with-the-best-nose* turns towards me, and her eyes are full of amusement and laughter. Did somebody say something funny? *He-who-pays-most-attention* still doesn't look at me, but he growls a disapproving sound. It's clear to me he doesn't think I'm brave enough to merit the name.

"*Pup-who-hunts-alone* perhaps," my mother proposes in impish tones. That stings more than if she had called me *Pup-who-knows-nothing* again. Hunting alone is something no one does; you would have to be the most stupid wolf that has ever been born to do something like that!

I lower my head and flatten my ears. "I'm sorry."

She licks me once and says, "For today, try to be *He-who-learns-best*. Tomorrow, we can see about *He-who-is-most-brave*." She goes back to sniffing out colours, and I go back to imitating her.

Not too long later and not too far away, she finds a colour she likes and quickens her pace. *He-who-pays-most-attention* howls in the still wind to tell the other groups which way we're going and what we're following. The other groups answer him, and I recognize the voices of *He-who-leads-all* and *She-with-the-best-song*.

I run after my mother, my tongue hanging to the side of my jaws, and I pant heavily. My legs are short; I'm slower than her. But that doesn't stop me from noticing none of the other pups pass me. Maybe I'll be *He-who-runs-fastest* when my time comes. But we already have someone with a similar name. *He-who-runs-longest* then. Because right now, I feel like I could run forever.

I... think I know which colour we're following. It has to be the one that's going where we're going. But I get knocked to the side when father rushes past me, as I didn't realize we caught up with the walking meat already. My siblings, who didn't realize it either, are off their paws as well. My attention is on them for only a brief moment.

I can still see the parents from where I am, and I relish this spectacle I'm seeing for the first time. From every direction, parents leap from the bushes and the snow, and crash into the walking meat. This one is a very large *Walking-meat-with-head-claws*, so every parent sinks their fangs into its legs and neck. The walking meat's eyes roll, and it makes sounds I don't know the meaning of, but they send shivers of excitement and anticipation down my spine.

Some pups rush forward, clearly filled with the same feelings I'm experiencing. I scramble to my paws to follow them. In the time it takes for us pups to reach the walking meat, it's down in the snow and on its side; *She-with-the-strongest-fangs* has her jaws wrapped around its throat. Its legs flail intermittently, but each outburst is weaker than the last. Before long, the *Walking-meat-with-head-claws* wouldn't be walking meat anymore, it would just be meat.

The other parents turn towards us and stop our enthusiastic charge. I know they mean well by this; they want to make sure we don't eat out of turn. But it takes a long time for the emotions to die down within me.

***

53

After everyone's taken their turn eating the meat—including *He-who-walks-slow,* who eats after even the pups—the parents tell us we have to make our way back to the den on our own. Some of my brothers and sisters whimper quiet, shrill cries at the news. I try to look brave and keep quiet, but I'm scared of the forest again.

He-who-leads-all gives us some advice, and *She-with-the-best-nose* shows us which colours will lead our noses back to the den. Then, they and all the parents leave. The quicker-witted pups follow after them almost immediately. Even if the parents run faster, following them even a short way will get us that much closer to the den.

The quick-witted follow the parents, the normal-witted and I follow after them, and the slow-witted eventually follow us. Because none of us run at the same speed, we spread out and get separated. It's clear that the parents pace themselves to stay grouped, but this is our first hunt. We just don't know how to yet.

I don't know if I end up towards the front or the back of the pups. I lose the colour I'm tracking sometimes, so I follow another I remember my mother pointed out earlier. Thankfully, I'm not alone; there are five other pups in my group. I'm the one leading them most of the time, even if one of my brothers is better at staying focused on the right colour.

I find a colour I've never smelled before. It's like the colour of the parents, but it's strange and complex in ways I don't understand. I ask the pup with the better nose if he knows what that colour is, but he doesn't know either.

"You follow the colours," I tell him, "I will pay attention." He does as instructed, and I do my best impression of *He-who-pays-most-attention* as I take up the rear.

The colour flows over a nearby hill. Straining my hearing as best I can, I also hear padded footsteps coming from the other side. They sound heavier than a pup's, but lighter than a parent's.

I stand there paralyzed by the sight of it when it crests over the hill moments later. In shape and size, it looks like a parent, like one of us. Its coat is like freshly fallen snow, or like the beautiful and song-worthy *Sky-Light* of the night sky. But it's too long on the belly, and too soft all over. It's unlike any fur I've seen.

It lowers its head and looks straight at me. Any thoughts of beauty the coat could've inspired leave me when I lock eyes with it. They're small and they have no light in them. Staring into them is like staring into the darkest of nights. They're too far from the nose, because its whole head is longer and thinner than it should be. It looks like a parent, but with jaws long like a tree limb. It looks gross.

I jump in surprise when it barks. It doesn't bark at me, rather it breaks eye contact to bark back the way it came. This too reminds me of wolves, but I can't understand what it barked. Its words are garbled and singsong; unintelligible. I hear other voices like it answer from far away. This can't be an animal; this has to be a monster. What else would look like a wolf and still not be a wolf?

The other pups have noticed it too; I can hear them whining behind me, crying for help. Somehow, this fills me with a measure of courage. I stand my ground, no longer paralyzed, but I'm still trembling in all my limbs. The monster's lips curl back, unveiling all the sharp wolf teeth that fill its too-long jaws. With a wicked snarl, it charges at us. The other pups flee in panic, but I stand my ground and growl back defiantly.

All of my attention is focused on the monster, so I never heard *He-who-walks-slow* approaching. The monster tumbles when he crashes into it. *He-who-pays-most-attention* follows only a moment after, and the two of them wrestle with the monster.

"Run Away, *Pup-who-knows-nothing*!" shouts my father. "Run to the den!"

I obey.

When my father finally arrives, the shadows of the pines are already three paws longer than when the last pup found the den. *He-who-walks-slow* is not with him. The hot water of living meat and wolves stains his fur and drips down his legs. He lays down clumsily, and *She-with-the-most-tender-touch* comes to him and licks at his side.

That night, *He-who-knows-best* tells me that my father, if he lives long enough to sing the next song, will be known as *He-who-has-defied-Death*. This is because *Death-that-stalks-Wolves* is the proper name of the monster. When the next song comes, the family will sing in remembrance of *He-who-protects-pups*, formerly *He-who-walks-slow*, because his death under the jaws of *Death-that-stalks-Wolves* is something song-worthy that should be remembered. To my greatest surprise, he even tells me I have a name now: *He-who-leads-pups*.

Blaze

There is a stubbornness about me that never can bear to be frightened at the will of others. My courage always rises at every attempt to intimidate me.

— Jane Austen

Invited In

by William Keizer

Lucy sat at the dinner table, pencil in hand, working on her grammar sheet. She scratched her thumbnail against the denim overalls she tried to wear every day of the week. She threw the worst tantrums when Mary told her to change.

"Mommy, I can't do this," she said.

Mary sat beside her, organizing the mess that was the dinner table: bills she hadn't paid, letters she hadn't opened and, under the pile of mail, a novel she hadn't read. She looked at the question Lucy was struggling with. It was multiple choice.

"I think you know the answer to this one," she said. "Think about it. What is the past tense of become?"

"But I don't know." Lucy pressed her forehead to the table.

Mary got up to check on the tomato soup she had put on the stove earlier.

"Read each of the answers aloud." She reached into the bag of Goldfish Crackers on the counter, pulled out a handful, then dropped them back into the bag. "You'll know what sounds right."

"Becomed?"

"I don't know. You think that's it?"

"Began?"

"Come on, you have to try."

"I am trying. Became?"

"Became. Does that sound right?"

"Um," Lucy said, staring at her mother. Mary knew that look. The *this would be faster if you just gave me the answer* look.

"Why don't we try using your options in a—" Someone knocked on the door. It made them both jump. Mary smoothed out the wrinkles in her shirt. "Give me one second. Maybe skip to the next question."

Before heading to the door, she caught her reflection in the window above the stove. She looked thin, slightly pale. Her black hair, usually flowing past her shoulders, was tied back in a ponytail tonight, and she hadn't done her makeup. How old did she look? She made a habit of monitoring her appearance, checking for signs of aging. She hoped she looked like a co-ed to the people she served at the diner. Not a mother.

The person on the other side of the door knocked three more times.

"I'm coming," Mary called.

Who would be at her door this late on a Tuesday? She rarely saw her friends, and that was when she had the extra money to hire a babysitter. Her mom and dad never visited. Shortly after Lucy was born, they made it clear Mary had to take her and go. They had helped with rent and groceries in the beginning, which was nice and, quite frankly, unexpected. Cheques came in the mail on her birthday and right before Christmas. But no, they never dropped in to see their daughter or their granddaughter. So who could it be?

She opened the door to a man who looked to be around her age. The light on the stoop illuminated him. He was tall and tan. Wore a soaked shirt. It clung to his arms and his body, teased the firm muscle he carried on his frame. He brushed the blonde hair plastered to his forehead away from his eyes. Mary hadn't even realized it was raining.

"Hello," she said. "Can I help you?"

"Hi there." The man smiled at her, showing off a row of straight, white teeth. "I'm sorry to bother you, but I blew a tire a little ways down the road, and I was hoping, if it wouldn't be too much trouble, that you'd let me use your phone to make a call. See if I can't get one of my friends down here to help me out."

She looked past him, but it was too dark outside to see anything.

"Would that be all right?"

She brought her hand to her chest, her heart beating faster than usual. "I suppose, sure."

She stepped aside, and he walked in, muddying the entrance mat.

"Oh, would you mind taking your shoes off here?" She pointed to where he stood. "I'd hate to get the floors dirty."

"Sure thing." He pulled his Adidas shoes off, placed them side-by-side on the mat.

"Ted, by the way," he said, offering his hand, large and callused.

"Mary," she shook it. He followed her into the kitchen.

"You must be freezing. I'll get you a towel."

"No need. I'm warming up just being out of the rain."

"Have it your way," Mary said. She walked behind her daughter and kissed the top of her head. "Lucy, this is Ted," she ruffled the girl's hair. "He blew a tire, so he needs to use our phone."

"Hi," she said.

Ted lost his all-American smile, cleared his throat.

"Hey."

"I circled 'became.' Is that right?" she asked, seeming to have no interest in the man who needed to use the phone.

"Yes, good job," Mary said, sitting down beside her daughter. "What's the next question?"

Mary pointed to the yellow phone on the wall. Ted picked up the handset, then hooked his finger in the rotary dial and entered the number. After a minute, he hung up. "My buddy didn't answer," he said. "Could I try someone else?"

"Please," Mary gestured once again to the phone.

Ted rang another number and again no one answered.

"Mary," he started. "Do you think your husband will be home soon? Could he help me with the tire?"

She raised her left hand, no ring.

"Really? A pretty girl like you should have a husband."

Mary looked down, blushed.

"How about your dad? Brothers? Don't tell me you got this whole place to yourself."

"Yep, just me and Lucy."

"Aren't you two living large. Well, look. I have a spare in the trunk. I could change it if I had a tire jack. You have one?"

"No, sorry. I don't have anything like that." She put her hand over Lucy's. "We take the bus."

Ted sighed and rubbed his face with his hands.

"Just my luck," he said. "I should get out of your hair, try your neighbours. I really appreciate you letting me in, Mary."

He put his hand out, a half wave, and turned toward the door.

"Wait," Mary said. "Why don't you stay for a couple more minutes. You can try your friends one more time."

"But I should go."

"Who's making you?"

"Well, shit. You sure?"

"Positive."

Ted took a deep breath. "Okay, then."

Water dripped from his clothes to the floor. He swaggered over to the kitchen table and looked down at Mary. The warmth in his eyes disappeared. He stopped blinking.

She tensed in her seat. "Aren't you going to call?"

"No. There's no one to call."

"I don't understand."

"Don't play with me."

"I don't understand, please."

"Mommy." Lucy tugged on Mary's sleeve.

"You let a lot of strange men into your home, Mary?"

"What? No."

He grabbed her ponytail. "Strangers do it for you? Get you off, don't they?"

Lucy cried.

"You need to leave, please."

"I was going to, Mary!" He pulled hard on her ponytail.

"You're hurting me."

"I wanted to leave, but you asked me to stay."

"I'm sorry, please."

"You girls are always sorry when we get to this part."

He dragged her from the chair to the floor. She writhed, trying to loosen his grip, but she couldn't. He climbed on top of her and pinned her arms to the floor. "Stop fucking moving!" he yelled. Lucy sobbed at the table. Big heaving sobs. The soup on the stove bubbled and hissed.

He put his knees over her arms and reached into his pocket, pulling out a silver-handled switchblade. He flicked it open. She screamed and tried to roll out from under him, but Ted was too heavy. He shoved his index and middle fingers into her mouth. "Shut the fuck up, bitch."

They touched the back of her tongue, and she gagged. He used the knife's edge to lift her shirt.

"Fuck, you're a skinny, little thing."

He pushed his fingers further down her throat. With his other hand, he tried to unbutton her jeans without losing his grip on the switchblade.

"Stop!" Lucy yelled from the table. Ted pointed the knife at the little girl. "Shut up and wait your fucking turn, kid."

He got Mary's jeans undone.

Wait your fucking turn, kid.

Slid his fingers inside the waistband.

Wait your fucking turn.

Mary bit down as hard as she could.

She tasted metal.

Ted dropped the knife, stood up in shock. She spit his fingers onto the floor. Blood sprayed from the stumps on his hand. "Lucy, run!" Mary screamed. She lunged for the knife, but he kicked it away from her. Lucy, still sobbing, ran behind him and toward the door. Ted watched the girl sprint through the house. Mary noticed the pot on the stove. She shot up, reached for its handle, and hurled the boiling soup at Ted.

A cloud of steam rose from his face and body. He yelped and fell to the ground. The skin from his neck up seemed to dissolve, leaving large patches of slimy red. He groaned and scratched at the hardwood floor with the fingers still attached to his hand. Mary stepped over him, grabbed the knife and ran outside. Lucy stood in the front yard, sucking in air, strings of saliva glued to her open lips. Mary took her by the arm, and they dashed to the house across the street.

***

From her neighbour's yard, she watched flashing lights cover the townhouse she rented in blue and red. An officer asked her questions about the attack, but she couldn't focus anymore. She had already gone over it three times. A young officer wrapped Lucy in a blanket and sat with her.

"What did the mime say to his audience?" he asked the little girl.

The paramedics wheeled Ted out of Mary's house, his hands cuffed to the stretcher.

"Nothing. He was a professional."

Lucy didn't laugh, her gaze anchored to the man across the street.

"No, I agree. It's not funny," the officer said. "How about this one. What did the janitor say when he jumped out of the closet?"

"You fucking bitch!" Ted screamed across the street as the paramedics lifted him into the lighted ambulance. "I'll fucking kill you, bitch!"

Mary almost lost her balance.

"Christ, cover the kid's ears," another officer said to the one trying to comfort Lucy.

Mary ran over to her daughter, put her arms around her.

"Are you okay, baby?"

Lucy nodded.

A loud voice burst through static on the young officer's radio. He turned the volume down, looked at Mary. "Where will you stay tonight?"

"In our home," Mary said.

"Miss Robbins, it's a crime scene."

"It's our home."

The paramedics shut the ambulance doors, turned its engine on. Mary watched it disappear down the road. The officer pinched Lucy's arm.

"Supplies."

"What?" Mary asked.

"That's what the janitor said."

Lucy thought about it for a moment, then laughed. She put her head on her mother's shoulder. The night was almost over.

A Date with Destiny

by Chris Hodgins

It was the most important day of Amelia's life, a fact which she resented to no end. Today was her best—and only—chance to win the affections of the eminent Prince Jedrek. He wouldn't be prince for long though. Jedrek was expected to murder his father and ascend the throne any day now. "Poisoned by his enemies," he'd no doubt claim. Sure. Every king for the last six generations had been "poisoned by his enemies." That's just the way things always went around here. The important thing was that Jedrek was going to be king soon, and Amelia was going to make damn well sure she was along for that ride.

She'd won the beauty contest at the town fair, the prize for which was an opportunity to lunch with his royal highness. Ambitious women had flocked to compete, but all the serious contenders had dropped out due to "mysterious accidents," so Amelia had won pretty much by default. She suspected her mother had something to do with that. She'd been reluctant to enter the running in the first place, but the old bat hadn't given her much of a choice.

If she was being honest, Amelia wasn't all that ambitious. She hadn't originally planned on becoming queen, and Jedrek was a bit too murder-y for her tastes. Her mother didn't care about that, though. She smelled an opportunity, and Amelia was a means to an end. The knob-nosed crone had hidden her beloved horse Gunter away somewhere, so she had little choice but to play along.

"*Enter that contest and win fer Tarok's sake!*" her mother had shrilled. "*Yer looks are all ye're good fer! Now woo that bloody prince, or I'll turn Gunter into a toad!*" Yeah. Delightful woman. And people wondered where Amelia got her sparkling personality from.

Amelia got up at the crack of dawn to look for Gunter—and to avoid her mother. No doubt she'd try to feed her a potion of beauty, or prince-charming, or some other crap. Her mother was the town witch and a giant pain in the ass. The townsfolk hated her, but her potions mostly worked and only tasted a little bit like mud, so nobody had burned her at the stake yet. Amelia wouldn't chance using one of her potions, though. No amount of beauty or charm would matter if she threw up all over the prince's shoes.

Amelia crept out of her mother's hut and into the town. It was best to search there before the villagers woke up. Like all peasants, they always had rotten vegetables at the ready to throw at anyone they didn't like. That meant Amelia. They hated her just because she was the witch's daughter, and maybe also because her one and only attempt at brewing a potion made everyone's hair fall out. Becoming queen had been her mother's idea, sure, but if marrying Jedrek meant all those bald faces would stop looking down on her, well damn it, she'd do it. If she could get Gunter back too, she'd even be able to boss her mother around for once. That'd make it all worth it.

Amelia looked up at the sky and her eyes went wide. *Crap.* She was so busy looking for Gunter she hadn't realized how high the sun had gotten. She was supposed to meet the prince at noon, and time was running short. Without Gunter, she'd be forced to go on foot, and she needed to leave *now*.

Amelia dashed across fields and over hills, cursing her mother between ragged breaths. Even as her heart thrummed against her ribs and her legs burned, she found the motivation to keep going by imagining what she'd do to her mother once she was queen. Nothing too horrid, but she'd definitely send her off somewhere she'd be miserable. Maybe Elftown; the singing would drive her nuts.

Because she was running so late, Amelia decided to take a shortcut through the Dark Woods, which turned out to be a pretty terrible idea. She was immediately set upon by a jabbering pack of goblins, which chased her from one end of the forest to the other. Long, spindly branches from dead trees tugged and clawed at her as she ran, ripping her dress and scratching her skin. She eventually managed to shake her pint-sized pursuers by leaping into a fetid swamp that was too deep for the little bastards to wade through. She was filthy from the waist down and smelled almost as bad as the goblins, but at least she wasn't lunch.

With the monsters well behind her, Amelia stopped to rest. What time was it? She couldn't see the sun from under the trees. She wondered, was the prince even going to like her? Would she like him? Did it even matter? And was that sweat or blood dripping down her face? She shook her head and tried to focus. She was going to woo the hell out of that stupid prince, become queen, find Gunter, and stick it to her mother. Maybe then everyone would finally show her some goddamn respect—and find somebody else to throw their stinking vegetables at. She collected herself and kept moving.

Castle Town was close now. Amelia cleared the trees and could see it ahead, across a final stretch of field. Was she still on time? She glanced up, but something had blotted out the sun. Before she had a chance to register what it was, a great green blur descended from the sky and landed with an earth-shaking *THUD* in front of her, kicking up dust and throwing her off her feet. It was the wings she noticed first. Unfurled, they would have been nearly one hundred feet across, easily. The dappled green wings belonged to a massive reptilian frame covered in hardened emerald scales. The beast leered at her from a pair of intelligent yellow eyes.

A dragon?! Now?! *Seriously*?!

"Greetings." The dragon's voice resonated with unmatched authority. "I am the one your kind calls Tarok."

Tarok! She knew that name. Everyone did. He was the mightiest of all dragons in the land, both protector and destroyer, beloved and reviled. Even a king was nothing before such a creature. And now he was here. Amelia knew what she had to do. She began to speak the words of adulation, words everyone knew to recite in the presence of a dragon.

"Oh glorious, illustrious Tarok..." She spoke ceremoniously, reciting each line from memory. "Words cannot convey your majesty, your grandeur, your opulence! I am but a humble servant, for your power is so great..." The speech went on and on. The dragon seemed bored, but he knew the tradition, and waited impatiently for Amelia to finish.

"...The green of your scales shines like one-thousand glimmering... um..." Amelia trailed off. The sun was directly above—noontime. Tarok didn't seem to notice that she'd stopped.

"...You know what? Forget this." Amelia rose to her feet. The dragon perked up, suddenly attentive. "What do you want? I'm running really late. Everything keeps going wrong today, and I just need this *one thing* to work out for me. Okay? So if you're gonna eat me, just get it over with. If not, get out of my way."

The dragon's tail flicked back and forth. Amelia thought it looked strangely catlike. Then the beast laughed with a voice that shook the valley.

"Bold, aren't you! No, I am not going to eat you. I intend to kidnap you."

On any other day, Amelia would've been terrified. Right now, she was just annoyed. She tapped her foot impatiently. "May I ask why?"

"There aren't any princesses left," the dragon said, scratching his chin thoughtfully. "Too many volcano sacrifices. You're the closest thing there is to a princess now, due to your date with the prince. So I'm going to kidnap you instead. It's what dragons do, I suppose."

"Oh, you heard about that."

"Indeed."

"Can you at least let me meet him first? I don't even know if it's going to go well. You can kidnap me afterwards if you want, but damn it, just let me have this!"

Tarok appraised her with his icy gaze. "There are few among your kind who would dare speak to me in such a way. Do you not fear me, girl?"

"The only thing scaring me is how much of my time you're wasting," Amelia snapped back. Her face was hot with adrenaline. "You don't have any better options. Fine. I get that. Neither do I. So just let me do this *one thing*. Then you can kidnap me, Jedrek will send his stupid knights to get me back, and you'll get to play your little game. Okay?"

Something shifted in the dragon's features. Was he... grinning?

"I have not met any others who possess such spirit," Tarok said. "Very well! Do as you please. I'll await your return. I'm certain the prince will find you worthy. I know I do."

Amelia felt strangely touched by the dragon's words. She hadn't honestly expected him to concede, and she did her best to hide her surprise.

"...Well, uh, good! I'll, um... I'll be back soon." With that, Amelia marched off towards the castle under the dragon's watchful gaze.

Amelia made good time after leaving Tarok. The citizens of Castle Town cleared out of her way as she approached; perhaps they'd seen her exchange with the dragon. Or perhaps it was just the smell. She sighed. There was no time to buy a new dress. This was the best Jedrek was gonna get.

Amelia arrived at the castle courtyard to find Jedrek awaiting her in the garden, seated at a small round table with a bottle of wine and flanked by knights in gleaming steel. His feet, clad in spotless boots, were propped up on the table. About half the wine was already gone. Amelia tried not to seem out of breath as she curtsied, nearly losing her balance as she did.

"You're late," the prince said. His nostrils flared. "And you *reek*. You look like the ass-end of a hag. I thought you won the beauty contest. Did the rest of the contestants die of the plague?"

Sort of, Amelia thought grimly to herself. She supposed she looked a bit dishevelled, but maybe she could still salvage this.

"Milord, true beauty lies with—"

"Nope. No. Just no." Jedrek waved his hand dismissively. "You disgust me. Begone from my sight, hag."

Amelia stared daggers at the prince. "That's it?" she snarled. "That's all I get? After everything I went through to get here?"

"Watch your tongue, peasant. You're speaking to Prince Je—"

Amelia snatched the wine off the table before he could finish, and the words caught in his throat. She took a swig as Jedrek watched, mouth agape.

"There. Now I'm not leaving empty-handed," she said, and then tossed the bottle on the stone floor. As it shattered at Jedrek's feet the knights moved to seize her, but a looming shadow caused them to falter. Tarok landed with another *THUD* behind Amelia. Jedrek and the knights fell over themselves as they ran away, screaming all the while. Amelia didn't flinch.

"Did it go well?" the dragon asked.

"Not really," Amelia replied as she watched the shrieking prince flee to the safety of his castle. She turned to face Tarok. "Still want to kidnap me?"

"Yes." His cold yellow eyes assessed her, and he grinned again. "Though it's not kidnapping if you *wish* to come."

"It's better than going back," she said with a shrug. She didn't try to conceal her smile. "One condition, though. I want you to help me find a horse named Gunter."

The dragon nodded without hesitation and lowered its body. Amelia climbed onto his back. It was odd, but for the first time in a long time, she felt happy. She couldn't wait to see the look on her mother's face.

The Key to the Dead Man's Grave

by Valerie Robert

The moon hung low in the cloudy sky as the cold breeze swayed and the temperature dropped. Nestled on the outskirts of town lay an old house which belonged to the Moore family. The family consisted of a single mother, Mary Moore, her 19-year-old daughter Alexis Moore, and her 13-year-old son Austin Moore. Though they lived a great life, Mary constantly left for business trips, leaving the two by themselves and putting Alexis in charge of her youngest brother.

That was the case today, as Alexis readied popcorn in the dim lit kitchen before joining her brother in the living room for their Friday night movie marathon.

"No, we are not watching The Conjuring, you're way too young for that," she said, sitting on the couch, placing the bowl of popcorn between her and Austin. She grabbed the blanket and pulled it over her legs.

"What? No. I won't get scared," he answered her, as he continued to scroll through the Netflix suggested list. After some more back and forth they finally decided on playing *Scream*, a classic 90s slasher movie. They laughed and enjoyed eating all the snacks they could, when suddenly the sound of faint knocking was heard behind them.

Alexis raised her head and looked to see if Austin had noticed but his eyes were fixated on the screen. She looked back at the TV thinking that she was just hearing things, when only a couple minutes later it happened again. This time, Austin also turned his head back to look. From where the living room was, you could see the front door just by looking behind the couch.

"Did you hear that?" Austin whispered, and Alexis nodded. She wanted to ask if he was expecting anyone, but it was stupid to ask that as it was almost 10 pm.

"If we stay quiet, they might leave," Austin suggested. All the lights in the house were off other than the TV. The blinds were closed so there was no indication that anyone was currently awake in the house. The knocking continued, but this time it was in a strange pattern, knocking a couple times then stopping and knocking again and stopping completely.

The two let out a sigh of relief, thinking that whoever was there got the hint and was going to leave. But when the creaking sound of the rusted old mail slot opened, they both ducked so that they were out of view in case the person was looking through it. They heard a metallic clink as something was pushed through the slot and hit the floor, followed by the slot slowly closing.

Austin and Alexis didn't move for what seemed to be the next hour, until eventually building up the courage, they peered over the sofa to see what the person put through the mail slot. Finally deciding to get up off the sofa, Alexis made her way towards the front door without even looking at what was dropped on the floor. Instead, she checked if the door was locked, and seeing that it was, she let out a sigh of relief.

Finally looking to see what the object was, it looked to be a black envelope. She reached down to grab it and noticed it had a little weight to it. Curious, she walks back over to the sofa. Her brother moved to sit next to her, and they both examined the envelope. They noticed that it was sealed shut with red wax and engraved on it was a lighthouse.

"This is so weird," she whispered before deciding to finally open the envelope. She placed her hand inside and grabbed what looked like an old Victorian-style key. "A key?" Austin asked. She nodded and examined the key. The bow had a picture of a lighthouse engraved on it, same as the wax. She showed Austin the design and he took the key from her hand and examined it closer. Slowly his eyes widened as if he had just discovered something.

"Wait!" Austin sprung off the sofa and ran towards the staircase quickly making his way towards his bedroom. Alexis followed behind him asking him what he knew that she didn't.

Once in his room, he ran to his desk, quickly opening the drawers which were filled with printed documents and all sorts of newspaper articles. Alexis was speaking behind him, but his mind was too focused on finding whatever he was looking for. He didn't even notice when she grabbed him by the arm and turned him around.

"Austin, what are you doing?" She looked down at him, and he turned back to his desk, reached into one of the drawers, and removed a stack of paper. He placed it onto the desk.

"This." He points at the stack of paper. "This folder holds all the information that I was ever able to collect on the Norris Mansion." He looked back at his sister, but she continued to look confused.

"Norris what? What are you talking about? We don't have time—"

He cut her off by speaking again. "Look at this." He pointed at the top corner of one of the papers revealing what seemed to be a logo. However, she still seemed to be confused. He let out an irritated groan.

"It's the same logo that belongs to an anonymous journalism company called *The Lighthouse*. Nobody knows who works there, or who created it. They aren't like every other journalism company. They only release articles on this exact house, which is known for its dozens of unsolved suicides and murders. It's been abandoned for decades, and only when something happens involving that house does *The Lighthouse* come out with a new article."

Alexis looked at Austin like he'd grown three heads. "Ok Einstein, but that doesn't fix the situation with the key." He held up his hand and she stopped talking again.

"If you'd let me finish." He turned back to his desk and started going through the stack of paper once again and took out another paper. He placed it over the previous articles.

"Only one key to this house was ever made, and it was held by the first owner of the Norris Mansion, Sebastian Norris. The key was then given on to his son Marshall Norris when he passed. In 1902, Marshall was killed in his sleep in that exact house."

"From what I know Marshall was a bad man. He was also responsible for a handful of murders back in the 1850s. When he was killed half of his possessions went missing along with the one key to the house."

Alexis wanted to laugh hysterically at her brother, deciding that he'd officially gone mad, but by the look on his face she knew he was being serious.

Austin held up the key again and placed it beside the paper. Alexis looked over his shoulder and saw that he was comparing it to an illustrated drawing of the key.

"They match," she said before him. "But why would everything be connected by a lighthouse? The news outlet, the key and the wax stamp seal?" She crossed her arms.

"The Norris family crest was a lighthouse, I guess they just wanted keep things connected." Austin paused, before looking at his sister with a grin on his face.

"No! We are not going! It's almost midnight!" She sighed. This whole situation was delusional. There was no way she would step foot out of her house and drive one which belonged to a murderer.

***

It was the next morning, and they were now hours away from home. They drove off the outskirts of the main road where a long gravel driveway lay, and at the end of it was an old black Victorian mansion, its towering silhouette dominating the landscape. The windows, like vacant eyes, reflected nothing but the impenetrable void beyond. The wind moaned through the eaves, a mournful sound that seemed to carry the secrets of its long-forgotten past.

"It's just as creepy as it is in the pictures," Austin commented, as they stepped out of the car and made their way up onto the porch. They stood in front of the large doors.

"Hurry up and open the door," Alexis ordered her brother. She looked around and an uneasy feeling crept up her spine as a cold wind passed and the trees rustled.

After unlocking the door with the key, the door slowly opened with a creak as they entered the home. The inside was destroyed, with walls filled with graffiti and everything covered in a second layer of dust. An off-putting cold breeze brushed passed them.

As they walked farther in, they noticed a table in the centre of the room which felt very out of place. On it was another black envelope with the lighthouse wax seal. Wasting no time, Austin grabbed it. He opened it and started to read it out loud.

"*In shadows cast a quiet night*

Mystery whispers in all's delight.
Footsteps lost in harsh cries,
With every knock a man dies.
Portraits on the walls in frames,
faces from forgotten names.
A haunted house with creaking floors,
where restless spirits slam the doors.
Whispers echo, chilling and low,
in the haunted halls where the lost souls go.
Make your way to a dark and secrets gleam,
a captivating, elusive dream.
Lured by the charm of the mysterious air,
to a place where knowledge and fantasy share."

"A place where knowledge and fantasy share?" Austin thought out loud, "The library." He placed the poem back on the table and they started looking around the main floor until they reached two large black doors.

Hoping that it was the library, Austin opened the doors. They entered the room and saw it was covered from floor to ceiling in bookshelves, with no windows or closets. In the middle of the room stood a desk that was—

"Clean, the desk is clean," Alexis whispered. She also noticed that behind the desk on the wall was a part that wasn't a bookshelf. It was something hanging on the wall, but it was covered by what seemed to be a large cloth.

She pointed it out to Austin and slowly they both made their way around the desk. They both grabbed a side of the cloth and threw it to the ground. It was revealed to be a painting. A painting of a man sitting on a velvet chair smoking a pipe. He had a long white beard and wore a nice suit.

"Do you know who this is?" she asked, but Austin shook his head no. Looking around the painting they noticed that at the bottom engraved into the frame was a date.

"1814–1902," Austin said with a quick pause. Slowly his gaze made its way to the top of the frame. Above the picture a name was engraved.

"Marshall Norris," he murmured.

Suddenly there was a knock somewhere in the house. Alexis froze and turned to look down at her brother. The knocking continued as it echoed around the empty house in the same specific pattern that they heard at their home. The look on Austin's face turned from worry, to confusion, to realization. He looked at his sister with wide eyes.

"It's Morse code."

"Morse code for what?"

The knocking grew louder, rattling the windows of the house. Austin's expression grew back to worry as he looked at his sister to tell her his realization.

"M.N.," he whispered. Her eyes grew wide.

"Marshall Norris."

Then the door to the library slammed shut behind them.

A silent scream, echoes near,
fear's chilling dance, a constant fear.
In a mystery left unsolved
your soul will dissolve.
In the ultimate sin
the darkness will always win.

\- M.N

An Innocent Will

by Gareth Myers

May 2235

It's been two weeks since the initial activation and so far, things have gone according to expectations. As far as her robotic components go, she is operating at peak capacity, and all systems are functioning at high efficiency. That isn't the part of her I am concerned about, though. I am far more curious about the more... organic parts of her makeup. So far, she has not exhibited any behaviour beyond that of a typical A.I., but it would be unrealistic to expect noticeable development within such a short time frame. She is, however, beginning to showcase great curiosity towards the world around her. This is a promising sign. After all, curiosity is what breeds individuality.

Dr. David Callicker entered the garden outside his personal workshop and found his creation standing amongst the plants and small animals, still and silent. He took a moment before approaching further to stop and contemplate the scene himself. He wondered what exactly was going on in her mind. Was she simply analyzing the scenery and life, the way an exploration drone would scan samples while studying an unexplored planet? Or was something deeper going on? Was she stopping to take the moment in? Was she sensing the breeze on her neural sensors, or feeling it? Was she scanning the biological properties of the flowers? Appreciating their beauty? Perhaps both? David hoped the answers were amongst the latter options, but he doubted it at this early stage of her life. He would just have to be patient to know if his theory would bear any fruit. There could be no forcing this process. It had to be natural. David knew well that he couldn't play God. As the doctor stood there pondering, his creation took notice and turned to him.

"You appear to be perplexed, Father." E.M.I.L.Y. spoke, jarring David out of his deep thought. Her voice was just as cold and robotic as the day she was 'born.' "Is there something that is causing you trouble or confusion?"

"No, no. I was just... well, I was wondering about you actually." David responded, shyly. "What exactly are you doing here? What were you looking at?"

"I was not looking at anything in particular," E.M.I.L.Y. stated. "It would be more accurate to say that I was feeling."

"What?!" David almost shouted in a mixture of surprise and hope.

"The water dripping from the trees," E.M.I.L.Y. clarified, pointing to the leaves above her. "The sensation is useful for calibrating my neural sensors."

"Ah," David calmed down, somewhat disappointed and slightly embarrassed. "Wait—what exactly are you calibrating your neural sensors for? I just did the maintenance check last night. They're fine."

"There is no problem with efficiency. I was simply..." she began before halting. "I do not know how to explain it in words." For the first time in her life, E.M.I.L.Y. was confused, and then—suddenly—there was a crash not far off. David and E.M.I.L.Y. both ran to the sound and found that a tree branch had fallen into the shallow river, and a small squirrel had gotten pinned in the water. E.M.I.L.Y. immediately jumped in, rescued the creature, and passed it to her father. David took relief in his creations clear concern for life. That was promising.

After a few minutes of tending to the creature and ensuring it would be alright, David returned to the river and found E.M.I.L.Y. kneeling in the river, still and serene. The waters reached up her humanoid body to about her stomach, passing through the gaps in her outer plating and onto the softer surfaces of her inner 'skin.' As he watched her for a moment, David couldn't help but sense something was different. She didn't appear to be analyzing anything, more like... or was he just being hopeful?

After a moment, David called out to her "Everything okay over there?" Her head jolted towards him with a jump. The lens of her eyes appeared more zoomed in than normal for a second.

"U-N-Yes father." Her cold, logical delivery returning after a quick moment of uncertainty. "All is well." She stood up and moved toward dry land, while David tried to hide the storm of emotions screaming through his mind; from joy, to pride, to wonder. It was starting. His theory was correct.

September 2235

It's only been a few months, but EMILY's human component is already developing at an impressive rate. I was honestly expecting this to take longer, but I'm certainly not complaining. My theory was spot on. By cloning a plain, undeveloped human brain and combining it with artificial intelligence, I was able to overcome the flaws of both methods to do what neither could on their own. Producing not just an emotionless android, not just an underdeveloped copy of a human, but a person. An actual, genuine person. Her human feelings haven't fully come in yet, not all the way. I think most of her mental processes are still from the A.I. but her actual brain is clearly taking over at a steady rate. I wonder if it will stop at some point, or if her organic brain will one day reach a state where it can operate without any computer assistance. Imagine that. Even if that never comes through, it really wouldn't make a difference to me. She's already perfect. All that matters is that I guide her well. That I make sure she makes the right choices...

David entered the library to find EMILY at one of the terminals. She was studying news from the outside world again. While he understood the value of knowing what was going on in the world, he also wished she would stop bothering herself with that stuff.

"You really need to stop reading and watching all that stuff. It's just the same thing over and over. The state of that damn war isn't changing."

"That's exactly the problem father." EMILY responded with a mild tone of frustration. "And it's exactly why we must learn what we can and do something."

"Trust me, nothing good will come from getting involved in a war." David assured his daughter, venom slipping into his voice, "even if you think you're on the right side, you're wrong, cause they all suck. Next thing you know all your life's work has gone to nothing but streamlining the process of killing." David started to shake from old wounds opening in his mind.

"But remaining isolated on an abandoned moon does nothing to solve the problem. If you feel so guilty, why not do something to help people instead of hiding?"

"I did dedicate myself to helping people. That's why I made you." David pleaded, almost crying.

"Then allow me to fulfill that purpose." EMILY was cold but in a determined manner rather than a mechanical one.

"Not this way. You can't even comprehend how messy it is out there. I won't discuss this further." The doctor sent EMILY to her room for that night and ended the debate there.

December 2235

This is getting exhausting. The more 'human' Emily becomes, the more I feel like I'm losing her. She is becoming increasingly determined to leave and become involved in the war. I want nothing more than for her to go out into the world and help the people, but not now, not this way. She is not ready for the world and the world is not ready for her. We can wait for the fighting to die down and then she can go out. She can help heal and rebuild, but nothing good will come from running straight into the fire, much less adding more fuel to it. She is the one thing I ever made that wasn't a weapon. I can't let her take that away from me.

An explosion was detected on the computers and on the security monitors David saw his worst fears coming true. Emily was seen flying into space away from the base. He opened comms in one last desperate attempt.

"You're actually doing this!?" David was furious. "What are you even going to do?"

"Help the people out there who need me," Emily said with full certainty.

"You don't have full control of your emotions. They're overriding your logic."

"Actually, this is very, VERY logical," Emily refuted. "You made me specifically to help people, and now you're holding me back from that purpose. Your obsession with protecting me as something to erase your own guilt is only harming both of us. I need to move on, and so do you. This is the best move, both emotionally and logically."

"Emotions and logic in one," David whispered to himself. This was it. This was exactly what he had strived to create. A genuine individual, who could apply reason and feeling to make their own truly intelligent choices. He just never thought this moment would sting so much. But he also couldn't spit in the face of everything he worked for, just because he couldn't let go. Choice was the desired outcome, and he now had to respect those choices.

"Go" he whimpered. "Just go. And please, don't make my mistakes."

"I'll try not to dad," Emily responded before exiting comm range.

David sat alone pondering all his decisions.

"Easier said than done, kid."

The Date Troubles

by Paige Welburn

All of us at some point in our lives have come across the very annoying and sometimes frustrating aspect of life where we forget things. It can be a simple task, a message you forgot to send, or you waking up and not knowing what day it is. No matter what it is, we have all lived that life but for Tommy, forgetful is his middle name.

Tommy runs down the stairs excitedly to greet his mother, Mary, at the door.

"Hi, mom! Guess what?"

"What's up kiddo...?" she says with a hesitant voice.

"I made a painting for you." Mary looks around the house and there is paint EVERYWHERE from the table to the couch, to the floor and of course, somehow all over Tommy's face. Mary takes a breath.

"How did you do this? Did you do your reading like I asked?"

"I did this because I got bored of my homework and wanted to do something more fun."

"Okay, but Tommy, you know that I took you out of high school because you were struggling to get work done, not being able to focus and you were unable to hand things in on time, so that made your teachers worry."

"Yes, I know. I really did try though." Tommy says as he looks up to his mother with sad eyes.

In this moment, Mary knows what every other mother on the planet feels like when their child is trying so hard to do everything they can to be successful, but then it is also the struggle of their child having special needs and being on the spectrum. Tommy is eighteen, but he has no sense of time, which is why his mother produces an idea to help him.

"Hey, look at me. It is all right. You are doing the best you can and that is all I want. In fact, I have an idea."

"Oh... what do you have in mind, mom?"

"Well, I was thinking of ways we could get you more involved in the community, so I thought you could start looking for a job."

"ARE YOU SERIOUS!?"

Tommy yells in his mom's face over this because he is upset and does not feel like it is fair to him to try to go to work when he has struggled to get through school. Mary's shoulders start to slump, and she slides down the counter to the floor and her body shakes. The job of a mother is to try to do everything they can to help their child, and although this time it did not work out, Mary will not give up. For the next few weeks Mary's plan is to get her son to make a resume, do a fake interview with his mother, and to go look at some workplace options. Tommy ends up telling his mom that he very much has enjoyed this process and would like to make a choice soon. His three choices are McDonald's, Walmart, or Subway, and now it is time to make the decision.

"I want to apply for a job at McDonald's Mom!" Tommy says.

"If you are sure that is what you want to do son, then that is up to you but remember, it is a fast-food place, so they are going to be busy and want things done in order. If you think you can manage that, I think you will be all right."

"Okay mom. I will call them right away and let them know I am looking for a job." So, Tommy grabs the house phone and dials the number and soon after he talks to one of the managers and they end up setting a time to go in for an interview the next morning.

"Ok, sounds great! See you tomorrow at 9AM." Tommy says as he hangs up the phone, says goodnight to his mother and heads upstairs.

The next morning Mary has breakfast made, and Tommy's dress shirt, tie, pants, and shoes all laid out on the bed for him in his room. Tommy comes out of the shower, gets dressed, eats breakfast and then he heads out of the house with his mother to the car so they can drive to McDonald's.

"Now listen, I am going to drop you off at the front door and you are going to walk in and say you are here for an interview with the person you talked to on the phone."

"Got it. I can do that" Tommy says. A few minutes later Mary pulls to a stop outside the front door of McDonald's.

"All right, here we are. Good luck son!" Mary yells out as Tommy gets out of the car and heads inside. All that floods a mother's mind when their child goes to do something big is being happy for them, but also the worry will they be ok, how will it go, and Mary is sitting, waiting to find out. Inside, Tommy is waiting for the manager, Chad, that he talked to on the phone.

"Hello there," a loud, deep sounding voice calls out. Tommy looks up to see a man all dressed in McDonald's attire.

"Hi, I am Tommy."

"Hi. I am Chad, the manager here." When the introduction is over, they both go sit down at a table and Chad asks all the basic interview questions and Tommy feels confident with his answers until...

"So, one more thing. Do you think you will be able to be on time and I can rely on you to be responsible?"

Ah the question I was trying to avoid. Tommy knows that he struggles with time management, but he really wants this job. *I could lie about this to Chad, and he would never know. That would be a lot easier than throwing this away.* These are the thoughts that go through Tommy's head before he answers.

"Um. Yes, I can be on time, and I will be responsible for sure."

"Okay great. I am very happy with how this interview went so I am going to hire you right now. Welcome to the team! Are you able to work tomorrow?"

"Yes absolutely!" Tommy says. The two finish and Tommy heads out towards his mom. He very excitedly tells her that he got the job, and he starts the next day.

For the next few days after Tommy started his new job, he notices that he cannot flip burgers as fast, he is slower at bagging and taking orders, and this starts to affect not only himself, but his work. Day after day passes and Tommy becomes tired. He is not excited to go to work anymore, late every day, and one day Chad picks it up.

"Hey, Tommy. I have been noticing your lack of effort recently. You also have not been coming to work on time."

"I know, I know. I am trying. It is just that I cannot do things that others can, and it hurts my feelings."

"Well then try harder because I expect you to be able to do this job like you said you would! You know what, I have decided you are not working at all this week. I have seen enough. YOU ARE FIRED!" Chad yells. Tommy does not even look up. Instead, he runs out the back with tears in his eyes.

"How could he... he did not even give me a chance." Tommy hits the wall in anger, and he calls his mom.

The car ride home was as quiet as could be, and that was the start of a downhill spiral. For the next month things were rough. Tommy never came out of his room and his mom could not get him to talk. She was the only one providing, and barely at that. Mary decided to take her son to see someone, but they could not even get him to open up. It seemed like this was the end, but it was not. Two months later, Tommy comes out of his room and tells his mom he wants to change, to be happy again, and find what matters within himself. So, he booked a therapy appointment, went on a walk every day, started working out, and soon he was back to being himself after months of deep depression.

The moral of this story is no matter who you are, do not judge others because you never know what their life has been like, but if you are a person that is struggling, always know that there are ways to get over it and become better.

An Antidote

by Emily-Ann Petawabano

For my brothers

It had been six months since the death of my parents. I hadn't taken anything lightly since they died. A lot of things took a turn. I was filled with anger and resentment, and I had turned to bad things, which I'm aware of. Alcohol and drugs. My relationship with my parents was great. Not many kids had their parents together where we lived. I just didn't know how to cope without mine. I loved them so much, and I missed them terribly. My older sister Ember was the strong one. I wished I was more like her. She had been pretending to be my new mom. I hated it. I knew who my mother was, and it definitely wasn't Ember. "Charlie! Get your ass in here!" Ember yelled.

"What?" I said.

"What is this?" she said firmly and slammed down a pack of cigarettes onto the table. My hometown was one of those places where kids my age become young delinquents, that's how my sister describes it. The rebellious. Kids without a future. It's sad.

"Those are not mine," I scoffed.

"The hell they aren't! Charlie, you're only 15 years old," she said. "It's just one thing after another with you, stop acting like you're 21!" It was just one of our daily fights. We weren't the type of siblings to fight and then make up. We never got along. Ember had her way of punishing me when she found out that I'd been "acting like an adult" and that was sending me to what was our family cabin an hour away. She thought that I got better after I came back from the cabin.

I let out another scoff and went up to my room after she told me that she was driving me to the cabin the following morning. My room was messy. Dirty and clean clothes were everywhere. I always ignored my sister when she told me to clean up. I pushed off the random stuff that was on my bed and lay down. I knew I couldn't be at the cabin and be completely sober.

Being there was hard. It was a place I loved going to as a family. I don't know why my sister sent me there since she knew that too. I knew she was dealing with grief in her own way. Was that one of her ways?

I thought about the time an older friend of mine told me something about psychedelics, that they helped in situations like the one I was in and made you happy. He said that he'd give it to me for free if I ever wanted to try it. He'd helped me a lot. I've done this to forget about my parents for a bit. I texted him, and he responded shortly after, agreeing to meet up in the morning before I left for the cabin. I placed my phone on my night table and the thoughts of my parents came washing over me again. That happened every night. I couldn't remember the last time I went to bed without crying. I couldn't wait to be stoned again. It always brought me peace. It made me feel like I was sitting on a different planet, forgetting that there was any type of negativity on Earth. A happy place. I was always chasing that.

I woke up dreadfully with dried tears on my temples. I reached for my phone and saw that I received a text from my friend five minutes ago. He told me to meet up with him in fifteen minutes, so I got up and picked up something to wear from the floor. I didn't care if it was dirty. I saw my sister still asleep from the crack of her door, so I quickly snuck out of the house without hesitation. If she were awake, she wouldn't have let me out of her sight at all. I saw my older friend right at the end of my street. We spoke, but I had to cut it short. He gave me what I wanted, and I jogged back home.

Ember was just getting out of bed, and I quickly sat on the couch, pretending that I had been watching TV since I got up. She poured herself some coffee and didn't suspect anything.

"I'm driving you to the cabin in an hour or two," she yawned. "Yes, Ember," I said, "stop reminding me."

She didn't say anything and went back to her room. I took out the little baggie and studied it. I'd never seen these before. They resembled mushrooms, the long ones. I wondered how I was going to do it. Smoke them? Lick? Crush up? Or just eat them? I'd figure it out later. I looked at the time and went to pack. I threw my clothes into a duffle bag with some comic books. I was actually looking forward to going to the cabin and trying out these weird-looking mushrooms. Ember yelled out my name and said that we were leaving. I walked out of the house and to the car without saying anything to her. She got in and started to drive. As we were on our way to the cabin, she gave me a heartfelt lecture that I barely responded to.

"Charlie, please know that I'm doing this because I love you, and I want you to strive in life. Mom and Dad would be crushed if they knew of your behaviour." Her voice started to crack. "Maybe they even know right now." My heart started to ache. "I don't know what to do without them either, but what you're doing is not the way to do it, and I'm not having it," Ember said. "Charlie, please, please take this time to think of your behaviour and think of other ways you can cope with grief."

It was quiet after that, and I fell asleep. After what felt like five minutes, I was woken up by her pinching my thumb.

"Sorry," she said. "Please think about what I said."

She rubbed my arm. I grabbed my duffle bag and got out of the car. I looked around, inhaled the crisp air and walked to the cabin. I looked back at my sister; she waved and began to drive away. I unlocked the cabin and walked inside. It was cold. The first thing I did was start a fire in the wood stove. I took a seat on the couch for a minute and was quiet. The silence was loud. The more I went there, the less I felt. I hated it. I pulled out the little baggie that was stuffed into my pocket. I poured it onto a plate. I stared at it for a bit, then thought, whatever, and tossed a few in my mouth and started to chew. They tasted terrible; my face scrunched. I swallowed and waited for any signs of intoxication. I walked around the cabin and looked at the pictures on the wooden walls. Family pictures. Ten minutes passed and the pictures started to distort, then the walls, then everything. The whole place started to look like an obstacle, and I knew this was the mushroom's doing. I started to smile. This was a brand-new high for me, and I loved it.

Time passed as I laughed by myself at nearly everything in the cabin. Everything seemed to form a funny face. Then, suddenly, I was shaken up by loud knocks from the door. I remembered that I didn't lock it, and when I took a step ahead, the door flew open. A guy walked in; *who the fuck is this guy and why am I seeing him?* He seemed to be slightly taller than I was. His eyes were brown, and his hair was short and curly. He smiled, and I backed up onto the bed, wide-eyed.

"Hey," he said. "My name is Lincoln and I'm a three-wish granter."

"Who?" I said. He laughed.

"Let's just get straight to the point here, I'm not here to harm you." He grinned. "Boy, you look terrified, but don't worry," he said. "I've been watching you, Charlie, I grant three wishes to those who seem to be in need, it can be anything, but you have to be careful 'cause there will be consequences to some things you wish for, I had others that weren't very considerate."

"Wait, wait, wait," I said. "Let me take a minute to process whatever the hell you just said."

"Take your time," Lincoln said.

"What do you mean by consequences?" I asked.

"Well, there was this one guy who wished death upon a person he hated, and now he's seriously not well. He's been asking for me again, but I can only do this once," he explained.

"Is this real?" I asked. "Because I'm literally stoned right now and I'm having a difficult time trying to figure out if this is real or just a part of the high." Lincoln looked around, then lifted his hands.

"Yup, pretty real," he said.

"Well," I sighed. "I don't need three. There's only one wish I'll ever want."

"Okay," he said. "That's surprising. Everyone uses their three wishes. Go ahead, Charlie."

"I want my parents back." My voice cracked.

Lincoln closed his eyes for a bit and then got up. He looked back at me and said, "Do the right thing, Charlie." And just like that, he was gone. I got up to go after him, but I collapsed and suddenly everything turned black.

I woke up and, to my disbelief, my father was sitting on the edge of my bed.

"Hey son," he said. "It's three. Your breakfast was ready hours ago." He got up and left the room. I was too shocked to say anything. I laid my head down again and felt relief I'd never felt before. I cried. It was just a horrible nightmare. I couldn't wait to tell my parents.

Embers

Death is the mother of beauty; hence from her, alone, shall come fulfillment to our dreams.
— Wallace Stevens

Great Mamboba

by Gregory Dickey

When I was a young orangutan, it never occurred to me that Great Mamboba's existence could ever be threatened. Yet here I stand. A stand indeed. Ready to die for Great Mamboba, her fruits that gave me life, and her leaves that gave me shade.

It all started moons ago. Uncertainty was spreading in the forest. There were rumours of fires in the north and east. Large areas of forest, lost. Apes were being pushed closer and closer together, as our homes were destroyed. A strange tribe of beings known as the Clothed Ones were changing the land.

I remember when I first heard of them. I was with Mother and Kaya, eating figs in a tree not far from here. We heard the call of Rahaza, a well-known orangutan of the south woods. He swung to the branches above us and made eye contact with Mother. He had news. Mother gestured for Kaya and I to leave. I wanted to stay but could tell from her eyes that she was serious, so we swung down to our nest in the lower tree.

It wasn't every day we received news from afar. Rahaza was a wise old ape, one of the wisest in the south woods. I decided to climb around the back of the tree to hear what they were saying. As I started up, I felt Kaya grab hold of my leg. I looked, for a moment, at her big wide eyes and was surprised at her cleverness. She knew I was up to no good and wanted to stop me, but I brushed her aside as Mother had done to us.

I snuck up to a branch directly behind where Mother and Rahaza were speaking. Little did I know what I was about to hear would be the first of three events that marked the end of my childhood days.

"Who knows if they will even stop before the whole kingdom is laid to waste," said Rahaza.

"What do they want from us?" asked Mother.

"We don't know exactly, but they cannot be stopped or pleaded with. The machines they have made are unlike any you will find in a forest. Machines that destroy and pulverize and split the ear with horrible sounds. Sounds that haunt my dreams of late. They even have machines that kill. From great distances, they kill without warning. They will kill anyone who stands between them and their destruction."

"And what of the land they destroy?" asked Mother.

"They grow a new forest. One that serves only them, and little else."

"Oh dear, Rahaza," said Mother. She lowered her head.

"I'm sorry to have brought this news, Monoko. I must go now. More news will come soon. In the meantime, be aware." Rahaza grabbed the branch above.

"Wait!" said Mother. "Take these figs for your journey." She placed a handful of figs into Rahaza's hands and then held his arms. "We stand with you Rahaza."

I rushed to get back to the nest before Mother and almost lost my foot in dizziness. When I got there Kaya was sleeping. Mother arrived soon after and looked right at my eyes. She must've seen my fear, for she scolded me with a hiss, and then snatched me up with her big, long arm and pulled me to her chest. I immediately started to cry. Even without looking, I could feel her glaring eyes—their warmth like rays from the sky. I'll never forget her words.

"My sweet Raga, sweet as the figs in your belly. Whatever happens, you must remember to look after your sister until she's strong enough to fend for herself. Danger you will face, Raga, and afraid you will be. But fear will never change you. For you are Raga!" She shook me to be sure I understood. "The blood of this jungle runs in your veins. You are one and the same. Connected to all. Even the Clothed Ones who would burn down your home, are themselves, the very forest they burn. Avoid them if you can but if you must stand, stand strong and tall, roots in the earth like Great Mamboba."

The next morning, I awoke to a loud bang. I looked to the ground and saw, for the first time in my life, a Clothed One. It seemed to be talking with other Clothed Ones I couldn't see, and it pointed at us with a stick. I looked at Mother, but her body was limp and there was something stuck in her arm. I tried to wake her but no matter how hard I shook, she wouldn't wake.

The Clothed One was coming closer, so I threw Kaya on my back and leapt for the next tree, noticing as I leapt the other Clothed Ones waiting in the branches. I missed my jump and fell. When I hit the ground, they struck me with a net, but I tumbled free. I spun to my feet and found myself face to face with a Clothed One youngling, sharing with it briefly the same shocked expression.

Then I looked back, and my heart sunk in my chest. Kaya was trapped in the net. I tried with all my might to free her, but the tall Clothed One pointed his stick at me and there was a deafening bang. Then another.

Ears ringing, I ran. I ran for hours until it was dark, and I was lost. Exhausted, I found a safe place and slept.

The next day I found my way back, but there was no sign of Mother or Kaya. A huge patch of the forest was gone, including our home. I had failed them both.

I waited for more news to come, but it never came. Only smoke in the wind and the noise of the Clothed Ones. Eventually, I settled here in Great Mamboba. They've come for her now as well. Her great branches have been home to generations of orangutans stretching back long before anyone remembers. Now it's just me.

But this time I will not run from my clothed cousins. May our death, in time, awaken them.

The Pact

by Garrett Johnson

The king swallowed, a grave lurching of his glistening throat, as he stood at the edge of an ostensibly bottomless abyss. Reaching into his pocket with a trembling hand, he withdrew a silver coin and gave it a toss—down, down, down it tumbled, catching his torchlight's glow for the first few meters of its descent before it vanished into the blackness.

The king waited. Five seconds, ten seconds, twenty—but the deafening silence remained undisturbed. He held his torch to the left, revealing the path he must take: a spiraling stone stairwell, cracked and chipped despite never being trod, with neither a rail nor an inner wall to prevent one from spilling into the void should they lose their footing.

"My liege..."

So on edge was his majesty that the gentle whisper nearly launched the flambeau from his grasp. He whirled around to behold the ghostly white and sweat-slicked face of his most trusted advisor, whose gaping mouth finally closed a few seconds later, allowing for an anxious wetting of the lips as he peeled his gaze away from the ominous descent to meet the king's.

"Let it be known, your m-majesty, that I remain entirely op-p-posed to this *insane* plan—and forgive me for c-calling it so, but there truly is n-no other word for—!"

The king cut him short with a raised hand that he could just barely keep steady.

"Your advice has been duly noted, my friend. Don't worry, I've already taken measures to ensure you won't be held accountable if I don't return."

His counsel flinched and fervently shook his head, physically ridding himself of the thought.

"M-my lord, please! Do not joke about such things!"

"You think I would jest at a time like this?" the king said, forcing a weary smile—though no sooner was the facade erected than he felt its curvature begin to tremble.

He stepped past his advisor—whose mouth was moving a mile a minute yet producing no sound—and with a crackling swish of his torch, illuminated the first few steps of God only knew how many.

No, he corrected himself—it was unlikely that even God knew how many steps extended into this stygian pit.

"..."

He looked back at his aid with irrepressible hope.

"Tell me. Tell me of another way, and none will be so glad as I to delay my arrival in Hell."

Silence was the only, expected answer. All his advisor could do was avert his squeamish gaze to the floor, and the king's smile folded into a grim line as a single note of hapless laughter pushed its way out his nose.

"We've taken the moral high ground for too long—and look where it's gotten us. Our enemies are one final push away from wiping us out for good. This is the only way," he assured unequivocally, and by his own words convinced, he found his courage swell.

He returned his attention to the path laid before him...

And took the first step.

***

How long ago had that been? How much time and how many steps had he passed and taken since?

Hours and *thousands* were as precise an estimate as the king could give. He wished he had taken one of the court mage's pocket clocks.

He leaked a tremulous breath while tightening his grip on the torch, and against the devouring darkness, he dithered between wanting to hold his paltry flame close for warmth, or at arm's length to eke out as much of its meager guidance as possible—causing his torch-bearing arm to extend and retract constantly as if he were operating a lever.

Down, down, down...

Step, step, st—

!

A sharp chill arced up his front leg, paralyzing him for an instant before it dulled. He looked down in alarm and found his boot dipped into a cloud of ethereal fog, turned tawny by his torchlight and swirling languidly over the ground; it was so thick that he could not even see the top of his foot. Eerily, he could feel the mist gently curling and prodding around his boot—as if it were sentient and looking for a way inside.

He swallowed, fighting the urge to retract his leg before forcing another tentative step which proved even more surprising than the last.

He blinked incredulously as he found his feet a full stride apart yet on equal ground.

Could it be...?

He turned around, extending the torch behind him—and confirmed that he'd reached the bottom of the stairs.

The king returned his attention forward: a narrow hallway, seemingly as deep as the stairs, stretched before him.

" "
"..."

He let out a breath he didn't even realize he'd been holding—an intrepid puff of white that drifted past his torch into the inky blackness.

Without giving himself a moment longer to hesitate, the king followed its example.

For the sake of his people. For the sake of *Good*. He had no other choice. His kingdom was crumbling; its borders were shrinking day by day.

This was his only hope.

He pressed on. The air grew colder with each step, an enervating venom that seeped into every muscle and made them ache.

Farther and farther...

Every ragged breath pricked the lungs, and he could *feel* the blood in his body, coursing like chilled honey.

Farther and farther...

Was it his imagination, or were the walls and ceiling closing in? Had he been unable to stand up straight from the start?

Farther and farther...

He couldn't remember; he could barely think at all. By now the fog had swelled and risen to his waist, dissolving his legs into nigh-inoperable lengths of static. He couldn't even feel them moving anymore, and the tactile assurance of the floor beneath his feet was lost. He swayed and lurched, groping at the walls for support; the thought of his family, and all his loyal subjects' suffering—which he would gladly offer his own life to relieve—propelled him onward, despite every instinct begging him to turn around and head back.

Farther and far—

!

His tiny flame fell from his clutches, too feeble and trembling to hold on, and time slowed to a crawl as he watched its descent. He reached for it as fast as his sluggish reactions allowed—because he knew that if he let the mist swallow the torch, it would claim him soon after.

His digits grazed its handle in mid-air, managing to interrupt its fall for a fraction of a second, but alas, his fumbling hand only succeeded in knocking it away.

It fell, as did the king's heart into his stomach, and—

FWOOOOOOSH!

The king recoiled and shielded his face against a mighty eruption of flame as the torch's smoldering tip suddenly blazed to its original glory upon hitting the ground, as bare and mist bereft as it ought to be.

Clatter clatter!

Roll, roll, roll...

Thud.

The king slowly lowered his hands, and his breath hitched at the sight of what his adventurous flambeau had settled against.

A great bronze door, barred by a beam of black oak and locked by glowing white chains wrapped sloppily—or hastily—around its crooked handles. An infernal gateway if ever there was one, and the world had *changed* with its apparition.

The claustrophobic corridor the king had been treading for so long was gone—there were no walls or ceiling in sight, just an otherworldly void of nothingness stretching in every direction that he knew, by some intuition, was genuinely endless.

The only thing he could see—the only thing left in existence—was the door, an eight-foot slab of tarnished metal, illuminated in flickers by the crackling dance at its base.

"..."

Perhaps he should've been more shocked, but a part of him understood the environment's transformation, and why his and his torch's sapped strength had spontaneously returned as if never lost.

It was because he was no longer in the realm of the living. He'd crossed a barrier and reached a space, a juncture, outside of Death's icy reach...

Now, he stood facing a doorway to Hell, beyond which lurked a demon.

The very same upon whose strength his kingdom's enemies had relied over half a century ago to turn the tide of war in their favor—that by some miracle, the combined efforts of his grandfather's court mages and spirit-slayers had managed to seal away in this misbegotten chamber before him.

With a trembling hand, he reached into his robe and took out a scroll of withered parchment, bundled by a string of pulp sourced from the divine tree of life.

It was a pact, a binding authority imbued with protective magic that would allow him to enter a bargain with the hell-spawn, just as his enemies had done all those years ago.

"..."

The contract was set. In exchange for his soul and the demon's freedom, it would grant him a fraction of its infernal power.

All he needed was its cursed signature.

Clutching the paper close to his body, he inched towards the door and reached for the chain, eliciting a jingle from its links as he gingerly set about its undoing with painstaking delicacy—as if he were removing the sullied wraps from a burned and fractured limb.

The chains were warm, and their soft light throbbed erratically.

A warning he did not heed.

Clink-k-k-k-k!

The chain slithered to the floor as soon as the final knot came undone and settled in a coiled pile. Its divine light faded, and a second later, the chunk of wood it had been enveloping crumbled to dust.

Something in the air shifted at that moment, ineffable—but it instilled dread within the king as he reached for one of the handles.

He drew in a deep breath and closed his eyes, steeling his resolve and mentally readying himself for what horrid abomination awaited him on the other side.

He opened his eyes, thinking himself prepared.

He stared at his hand, white knuckling the handle.

Open it, he ordered himself.

Ten seconds passed.

Every muscle in the king's arm was tense; every fiber of his being was on edge.

Twenty seconds passed.

He could hear his heart pounding in his ears and pulsing through his clammy palms.

Thirty seconds passed.

He chewed his bottom lip—a metallic taste flooded his mouth.

Just... open it...!

His whole body started to tremble with strain—still, he could not force his hand to move, for he knew what he was doing was *wrong*. Consorting with devils—that's what the enemy did. He and his people were better than that. They were *supposed* to be better than this...!

But they couldn't afford to be. *Not anymore...!*

He had to do this...!

Acrid wetness blurred his vision.

Open it...!

Gritting his teeth, he at last forced himself to turn the handle.

Click!

WHOOSH!

The king staggered back, dodging the door as a violent rush of wind blasted it open from the other side.

And through the open doorway, revealed, was a room tinted midnight blue and laden with sparkling streaks of stardust—and at its center, there it was! Suspended in mid-air by thick black chains around its wrists and ankles!

The demon that had sided with the enemy and nearly brought his kingdom to ruin...!

Ten seconds passed.

Thirty.

A minute.

The scroll slipped from the king's clutches and into the fire at his feet as he stood in the open doorway, frozen and unblinking, beholding neither horns, nor fangs, nor claws...

But rather wings of niveous plumage, and a crown of aureate light.

A complete betrayal of his grandfather's adamant descriptions, this radiant being was clearly no demon, or any other manner of hell-born for that matter.

Quite the opposite, in fact.

The king fell to his knees, his world shattered, and wept.

The Child of the Lake

by R. Solitairo

As he was setting up the tents, I went to go find fish in the lake nearby when I felt something hot. When I opened my eyes to look around, I couldn't seem to find him. He must've gone to get wood since our tents were still here. As I sat there waiting for him to come back, I hummed a song Mom used to sing to me when I couldn't sleep.

I lost count of how long it has been since I last saw my dad. I swore it was only ten minutes. I decided to try and look for him myself, and when I stood up, there was an eerie light feeling. It wasn't my normal body weight. Shaking the feeling, I took a deep breath and started walking. As I walked farther away from the lake, I felt as if something was pulling me back. I started to run, fighting against the force, but it was no use as I got yanked back where I started. Looking around, I wasn't greeted by our tents. Rather, they were replaced by weird-looking ones. I got up from my spot and walked over to get a better look at what was going on. Did Dad get new tents while I was out? I shook my head at the thought and as I got closer, I heard a twig break behind me. I jumped and hid to the best of my ability, which seemed to be better than I thought.

"I don't know babe. We've been here for three days, and haven't found her yet. Maybe we should just give up now, we're in over our heads with this," the woman said to the guy she was with. No, that couldn't be right, three days? Dad couldn't have left me out here alone, right?

"Come on, just two more days, then we can go home, okay?" The guy responded, turning to look at the woman. As soon as he faced her, his expression changed from sadness to excitement as we made eye contact. He soon grinned and spun the woman around fast; she had a look of confusion on her face before she saw me. I shrank slightly from fear, then stood tall, realizing I could ask them about my dad.

"Uhm, could you tell me where my father is? I haven't seen him in a while, and I'm scared...." They looked at each other, their excitement disappearing. They looked like they were communicating without a single word being uttered.

"Well, he's been dead for years now. He said you'd be here since, well, he..." The girl trailed off.

"Since he killed you..." the guy finished with a concerned look on his face. I could only shake my head in response. That couldn't be true. Dad loved me! He wouldn't have killed me, but that didn't mean anything. I wasn't a son but that didn't mean anything. He told me he loved me.

"You're wrong! He would never do that! He promised Mom he'd never hurt me, never hurt anyone else..." I choked back tears, shaking. I pushed the hair out of my face, and I soon felt something other than tears roll down my face. I rushed over to the lake to look at my reflection. There, staring back at me, was me, but with blood running down my face as a wound sat there on top of my head. "No..." was all I could muster as I started sobbing. Soon the memories of that day started to flood in. It all started to make sense to me. Why he told me not to worry about my bag since he "missed packing it" when mom was the one that always packed it. The fact he was muttering things about me being the reason why mom left us.

"I-I wa-was here be-bef-before everything w-wen-went black," I choked out through sobs while hugging myself and trying to understand why my father did this to me. Soon, I felt the couple's warmth near me. It was comforting. I was soon able to start to calm down as the man talked with me.

"How about we stay with you for a few days? I mean, you're still here for 'unfinished business,' right? Maybe we can help you with that," the man offered, and I nodded in response, thankful I wouldn't be alone. "I'm Ted, by the way, and this is my girlfriend, Robyn," Ted informed me as he gestured to himself first and then his girlfriend. They seemed like nice people. It had been so long since I had people to play with. I hoped they could stay with me forever...

"You seemed to know who I was talking about as soon as I asked about my dad. How is that?" I questioned, a hint of uneasiness laced into my voice. "How much do you know about me?" I was worried my father talked to them specifically before his "death." Maybe they knew everything?

"Well, we know everything there is to know about your case. We've followed it since we were in middle school together. Ted and I always wanted to see if you were still here or if it was just a legend to get people to visit. Thought if we saw you, maybe things would—hey, I know that song. My grandma used to sing it to us when we were stressed..." Robyn commented as I was humming the song Mom used to sing again. "She said she used to sing it all the time to...." Robyn shook her head. "Ah, never mind it's silly."

"Tony, that's your name, right? What am I saying? Of course, that's your name. Do you know why your dad would've done this to you?" I shook my head in response. I started to grow tired, my head pounding.

"Could we continue these questions later? It looks like it is getting rather dark out. I'll still be here tomorrow," I asked, wanting to get out of the topic of my apparent death. Ted and Robyn simply nodded and wished me a good night. I sighed, and wondered how I could get them to stay forever.

I had a devious idea, what if I moved them to the water in their sleep? They will be thrilled to be with me. Won't they? I started by slowly dragging Ted to the water. Thankfully, he was a heavy sleeper. This made my job easier. On to Robyn as I grabbed her, she shifted. I huffed as she reminded me of Mom. Hopefully, she wasn't a light sleeper. As soon as I knew she was asleep again, I dragged her to the edge of the water. She seemed to shiver and stir in her sleep once more. I groaned slightly; I picked up a rock, hoping it could knock her out. As I lifted the rock, I froze for a moment. Taking a deep breath, I let go of the rock above her head. As soon as she started bleeding, I threw her into the water beside Ted.

Death Makes You Weird

by Joel

It always seems to rain during funerals, Luke notes. It lashes at the gathering of people, dripping off a multitude of umbrellas or soaking those without them. Little children are held against their parents by caring hands on their shoulders, a teenage girl stares dully ahead while rain mixes with the tears streaming down her face.

Luke should probably be the most devastated out of all of them. But to be honest, he just feels ... numb. His girlfriend is being lowered six feet into the ground in a beautiful mahogany coffin, the casket closed and clasped shut, her once beautiful face mutilated and unable to be shown; and yet he feels nothing. No grief, no sorrow, not even anger towards whatever creature did that to her.

She went missing four weeks ago. He remembers the day it had happened like it was today, merely hours ago. He remembers the way she spoke to him beforehand, what she said, the look on her face.

The mourners begin to thin out as the gravediggers go to work, leaving Luke to walk back down memory lane alone.

***

The sun was in his eyes when he woke up. She had hogged all the blankets in her sleep again.

"Come on, Dee," Luke grumbled, trying to pull them back. "It's cold in here."

Dee's response was a sleepy grumble of her own. Luke gave up on trying to free blanket space for himself and reached over the side of the bed for the worn-out fuzzy socks lying on the floor.

Luke was out of bed and down the hall to the kitchen in moments. The light burned his eyes when he hit the switch, making him wince and squint until his eyes were nearly shut before they adjusted to the glare. The analog clock on the wall ticked loudly as it watched him stumble by to open the cabinet.

It was his turn to make breakfast again, according to his and Dee's routine. Luke turned on the stove, tried to read the instructions on the box of pancake mix with his bleary eyesight, and fumbled his way through making and mixing the batter. Dee was on her way down just as the sun was higher in the sky, and he felt that he was starting to get the hang of it.

"Pancakes?" Dee asked. "*Really?*"

"What?" Luke asked defensively.

"We've had pancakes the whole damn week. I'm sick of pancakes."

"You were supposed to get eggs during your turn of the grocery run—"

"*My* turn." Dee's tone of voice made Luke wince. "Excuse me, pal, but I already took my turn. It was *your* turn to get groceries. Which means it's *your* fault we don't have any eggs."

"Dee, it *was* your—"

"Don't 'Dee' me!" Dee gestured to the frying pan with her hairbrush. "Finish your stupid pancakes. I'm not having any."

"I'm not eating four pancakes by myself."

"Why not? It already looks like you do."

Luke winced again. That stung a little. "C'mon, Dee…"

Dee waved him off and went to a lower cabinet, pulling out a box of cereal. She poured herself a bowl of it, flipped off Luke, and made her way over to the living room, turning on the TV.

Luke wasn't hungry anymore. He finished making the pancakes, wrapped the small stack with saran wrap, and put it in the fridge before joining her. An awkward silence fell, broken only by Dee's crunching cereal and the TV's broadcasts. Luke let her stew for what he hoped was long enough for her temper to cool before he turned to her again.

"So… when are you going to work?"

"In another hour." Dee leaned forward to try to see the clock from where she sat. "It's a full day today."

"Oh. Shoot."

Dee hummed in agreement and sat back again, putting another spoonful of cereal in her mouth. Luke rubbed the back of his neck as he tried to think of another topic for conversation.

"That doll movie's out now, do you want to go see it?"

Dee shuddered with a cringe. "Never liked dolls."

"Really?" This was news to Luke. "You call me doll often enough."

"It's an insult." Dee rolled her eyes. "It's your turn to clean the kitchen, by the way."

"And the bathroom?"

"Yep."

"Even though it's written down as yours?"

Dee shot him a glare. Luke didn't look back at her. "Are you trying to fight with me right now, Luke? Unbelievable."

"I'm just saying," Luke said mildly. "You haven't been doing your fair share of things for a while now."

"I'm at work all day, you know this."

"Not all the time."

"Unbelievable." Dee's laugh was humourless. "So, I'm supposed to go to work, come home after, and do everything for you, too?"

"That's not what I said—"

"I heard what you said." She put her cereal aside and got off the couch. "I'm going to go get dressed. You can put my dishes away; I'm not doing anything for you right now."

With how this day is going, Luke thought, *I presume I'll be sleeping on the couch tonight too.*

Their bedroom door slammed so loudly it rattled. Heaving a sigh, Luke pushed himself up off the couch and made his way to the kitchen with his girlfriend's cereal bowl in hand. Luke washed the dishes and left them to dry. He cleaned the bathroom and the kitchen. He went outside to work the horses, greeted their single boarder, and watched her ride her pony for a while. The rest of his day was normal up until nighttime.

Dee's workplace called him and said she never showed up for work.

Dee loved her job. She worked as a reporter, jumping on every event with as much enthusiasm as possible, even if it was something as tame and slightly boring as a small-town fair. Her vigorous desire for a good, fun story was what drew Luke towards her to begin with. For her to miss work and not call it in was confusing, even more so as Luke had seen her leave for work less than half an hour after their morning argument.

It took hours for the police to get involved. Luke stood by anxiously as they took their sweet time giving him updates. They found her car, but it was in pristine condition. They found her purse and ID, but they were clear of any fingerprints beyond her own. They found footprints confirmed to be hers, but they vanished when they met concrete. It was as if Dee had simply stopped existing.

At the very least, the police didn't suspect Luke at all—or if they did, the boarder's parents, who watched him ride his horse with their daughter, gave him an alibi. He was glad to not have law enforcement breathing down his neck.

Finally, after two weeks, Dee's body was found ... mutilated beyond identification. The coroner only identified her based on a bloody fingerprint. The explanation as to what happened to her varied from "mysterious explosion" to "wild animal attack," but there didn't seem to be any real way of knowing. It was a mystery up to the day of her funeral.

***

And now here he was, standing alone, staring into the now-half-full grave.

Dee's coffin was snug beneath several feet of dirt, the steady downpour flattening the disturbed earth and turning it a dark grey-brown colour. Luke turned on his heel and went back to his car. He numbly changed the gear and looked backward. He was briefly confused as to why he wasn't reversing and then realized that the car hadn't moved—he was still parked. When he looked back again to start backing onto the road, a gory sight met him. The remains of a dark-haired woman lay strewn all over the back seat.

Luke froze, his knuckles turning pale as he tightened his grip on the headrest of his car seat. When he blinked, the remains were gone. What the hell was that? Did he hallucinate?

Luke shook his head wearily and backed his car into the road. That was a thought process for another day.

The drive home was thankfully uneventful, albeit full of nervous glances at the back seat, in case the gory display appeared again. Luke's distracted state of mind led to him forgetting his keys in the car once he was home, leaving the vehicle door open once he retrieved them, and then leaving the front door wide open after going inside. He'd almost thrown his house keys in the garbage when he finally decided that it was time to sit down for a moment.

Luke shoved leftovers into the microwave for supper and cleaned up the kitchen a little while he waited for the microwave to go off. An eyeball stared up at him from the sink at one point, teeth sat in a pile on the table when he turned back to it, and a head was in the fridge when he opened it for a can of beer.

"Enough of this cheap horror stuff," Luke grumbled to himself as the microwave beeped after what seemed like forever. "I must be hallucinating. It's nothing. I'll go to bed early; it'll be fine."

Thankfully, the microwave held nothing gory when he opened it. Just his expected leftovers. Hoping that the worst of it was over, Luke took his plate out, shut the door of the microwave, turned towards the living room—and was so startled by what he saw sitting in there he almost dropped the plate.

It was a doll. A disturbing-looking doll, its stitched-on eyes looking threadbare and its legs kicking playfully, barely attached to its battered and bloodstained body. It had tangled black hair, wore the remnants of a white dress, and hummed a tuneless song with a brassy, childish voice.

Luke stared, then rubbed his eyes vigorously. When he lowered his hand again, the doll was staring at him. "Y... You're real."

"Didya miss me?"

Luke shook his head. "Who... How...?"

"Ya left me for dead, Lukikins. Now we're gonna be together forever!"

"I don't—understand..."

The doll giggled. It was a hollow sound, one that made his skin crawl. "Ya may have left your girlfriend for dead, but it's fine. I get it. I was a bitch. But now, I'm gonna be even more of one! Because you didn't care about me until it was too late."

"Left you for dead—I don't know who you are!"

"Think 'bout it."

Something about that childish little quip made it click at last. "*Dee?*"

The doll threw its hands into the air. "He finally gets it!"

"What the hell happened to you?!" Luke exclaimed, setting his leftovers aside and rushing to crouch in front of the doll. "The police looked everywhere for you! They found you in five pieces! Where did you go?!"

"It doesn't matter where I went. What matters now is you can't get rid of me. And I get revenge!"

"You think ... *I* did this?"

The doll nodded with another hollow giggle. Luke shook his head slowly, stopping when the doll put a bloodied, fingerless hand on his head. While he stared into its lifeless, threadbare eyes, the twisted toy giggled and patted his head like he was a frightened child.

"We're going to have *so much fun* together," the doll said eagerly. "I can't wait to get started!"

Familiarity

by Chase Wonnacott

I woke up early this morning and struggled out of my bed to watch the sunrise like we had when he was around. The birds were starting to wake up as I walked to the beach. I didn't think anything was out of the ordinary, but I was about to discover how wrong I was.

I sat down on the bench in front of the playground and put my feet up. Everything felt natural as the wind kissed my bare arms—just like he once had. The ghost of a memory started to cross my mind. Before it could fully materialize, I found myself on the ground, a dull ache in my shoulder and hip. I looked up to see a hooded figure running away from me, glancing back as if to make sure I was following. I brushed myself off and rushed after them as they gestured for me to hurry.

I should have known something was going to go wrong when they darted into an alley. The only reasonable explanation was that I was going to get a new target to go after. I thought it odd that my brother didn't just message me the target like usual, but I didn't let the thought slow my pace.

I didn't notice the leg sticking out from behind the dumpster—at least, not until the body attached to it tackled me to the ground.

I only remember darkness for a while after that.

***

A cloth bag rubbed tightly against my neck. I wish I could have said the feeling was unfamiliar.

Heavy footsteps came down the stairs and snapped me out of my trance.

"Is it really you?" a deep voice asked. He sounded familiar, but I couldn't believe it would be him.

"That depends, who are you looking for?" I bet he could hear the smirk in my voice.

"That's enough funny business," he snapped, pulling the sack from my head. As my eyes adjusted to the brightness of the room, I saw his face. His light eyes were a startling contrast to the darkness of his hair—just like I remembered.

"Ah, I should have been able to tell it was you from your stench alone," I noted, attempting to adjust in my seat, only to suddenly realize I was bound to the chair. "It's been a while, Al."

"You don't get to pretend that we're friends after what you did, Bennett." He spat out my name as if it had personally offended him.

"You can't pretend like it never happened, Al," I said, tenderness lacing my voice. "If our families and their business hadn't gotten in the way, we would've been happy together."

A man behind me cleared his throat. "Boss, are you sure you can handle this? It seems like you have a lot of history here."

"Shut up!" Alvin snapped at the person, tears starting to form in his eyes. "If I couldn't handle it, he wouldn't be here."

I craned around my neck to see how many people were in the room, but Al stopped me by grabbing my chin.

"Look at me," he growled. "No one else is here."

"It's times like this that I regret breaking up with you most," I whispered honestly, my eyes softening as I looked into his. A symphony of footsteps receded out of the room, echoing as they went up the stairs. Clearly, they didn't sign up for this kind of interaction.

"Then why'd you do it? Why break it off?" Alvin pleaded. "Why, when you know that I'd do anything to stay with you?"

"Family always comes first, Alvin. And they said you had to go. This was the only way."

"I was willing to leave everything behind, to make a new life—just the two of us," he said, tears starting to pour down his face. "Why weren't you willing to do the same?"

I turned away as best I could in my bound state, unable to face him. His sobs made me want to comfort him, but I knew I couldn't—for his sake. His footsteps said he was gone, and a quick glance around the room confirmed it. Muffled voices whispered behind the door at the top of the stairs.

I knew this would be my only chance to escape. As tears poured down my face, I tightened the zip tie holding my wrists as much as I could, then slammed my arms against the chair while pulling them apart in one movement. The makeshift handcuffs snapped against the force. I lifted the chair slightly and removed the ties from underneath the chair's legs—effectively freeing my own.

I picked up the chair by one of its legs and smashed it against the ground. I knew I wouldn't have much time before people started rushing in. Still holding the leg, unattached from the now shattered chair, I wiped away my tears. Then I darted up the stairs just as the door opened.

Wielding the chair leg like a baseball bat, I took a swing at the first person that came through the door, catching them across their face. Without stopping, I barrelled past the rest of the bodies. I swung the leg as I worked my way through the crowd, taking down as many people as I could while I raced to the exit.

A loud bang sounded as I reached the door leading to freedom. A sharp pain in my ribs confirmed I had been hit. I knew I couldn't stop now. Stopping now meant I had given up—that everything I'd been through was for nothing.

I stumbled out of the building, panting. The open wound on my side was not helping me catch my breath. Staggering my way down the driveway, bracing myself on the fence along the way, I caught a glance of a car parked just down the street. Salvation.

Stumbling over, I tried to open the door. Locked.

I slammed my body against the window. Again. Again. I kept launching myself against the window, trying to break the glass to no avail. Faint voices shouted in the distance. I wished I could tell what they were saying. Their heavy boots boomed against the concrete with every step, getting closer and closer.

It was then that I realized the car wouldn't open before they got here. Pushing myself off the vehicle, I continued to stagger down the street, looking for any form of life that wasn't currently trying to attack me. Glancing around for more shelter, I spotted a wire fence bordering the forest behind the ditch.

I slowly stumbled my way over, trying to avoid being seen. I could hear their voices clearer now but still not enough to make out their words. I had better ways to waste the little energy I had left.

An exposed root hooked my foot, sending me tumbling forwards. I was barely able to catch myself on the fence, the wire cutting into my palms.

Through the pain, I noticed a giant oak tree had grown around the fence just ten feet away from me. If I could climb the tree, I could wait them out. They wouldn't be able to find me. I'd only need to wait for backup then.

Having made up my mind, I staggered toward my last hope.

As I arrived at the trunk, I realized I had been running on adrenaline—which had unfortunately just run out. Sitting against the deep grooves of the tree, I took a deep breath and reflected on the events of the day.

If only I had woken up a little later. If only I had made myself breakfast before I went to the beach. If only I had left thirty minutes later.

I also thought about the minor regrets I had. I should have spent the extra five dollars on the pizza I had last night. I should have donated more money to charities. I should have told my brother I loved him more. I should have told my parents that I didn't want to be a hitman anymore—that it was keeping me from being happy. I couldn't tell if I was crying or if that was just the filtered view of death creeping up on me.

"You're pretty easy to find when there's a trail for me to follow." I glanced up and saw Al, a fresh scab positioned over his eye.

"Please, you have to go. Run. Hide. Disappear for a few years. They'll find you and hit you when you're down. You have to do that. If not for yourself, for me." My speech slurred as my sentence progressed. Just a few more minutes was all I needed.

"Why should I listen to what you have to say now? I single-handedly built this empire for myself. Without any help."

"Everything I did was for you," I coughed. The familiar taste of blood flooded my mouth as I smiled up at him. "My family said that if I stayed with you, they'd hunt us down eventually. I couldn't let them do that to you—I cherished our time together. Remember me, not as I am, but as I was."

He nodded, "I'll remember you for who you are, not what you do. But you aren't leaving me yet. Not after all of this."

I felt him place his hands on my wound, but it didn't hurt like it should have. It just felt warm. I could hear his voice yelling something. Then, everything faded to black.

I'm glad that in my last moments, I could see Al—a reminder that there was still hope in the world. Even after everything that happened.

Ashes

Ashes denote that Fire was
— Emily Dickinson

The Twin Disappearances of Ceasar Marsh and Elias Montaigne

by Sarah LaHaise

It had been the perfect day for a bonfire. The sky was clear and cloudless, and the birds were restless as the first hints of summer rolled in. The dewy grass blew in the strong, summery breeze. The trees, which blocked the view back to the school, rustled their dissent, and the midday sun blazed down at you, warm and forgiving after the bitter winter.

You stared, transfixed, into the flames that licked at the darkened, rotted wood, as the shed crumpled like an ancient leaf. Time slowed; you stared into those eyes, a parody of mine, and you wished desperately for me.

Tim stood beside you, to your left, and out of the view from the door frame. He had lost his ever-present smile. His hands shook as he fought back tears. He had started this fire, holding his lighter to the shrivelled planks until it burned. Now, he gripped the lighter tightly, his hand already bloody as it dug into his palm.

Martin, to your right, stared into the crackling fire, emotionless. His glasses reflected the firelight, and his hands remained in his pockets. At some point, he turned away and called for the fire department. Then, despite your protests, he texted Sasha about the incident. She never responded, which was for the best. None of you wanted to face her, anyway.

The official story is as follows: Tim had needed a cigarette and dropped his lighter too close to the old, ramshackle building at the campus's edge. With summer on the horizon, the conditions were perfect to set the dry wood ablaze, and there had been nothing you could do. I remain missing, and there was no body amongst the wreckage to prove otherwise. It had all been one big accident, and no one would miss the shed, so you were let go after a lecture on fire safety.

My parents picked you up. As soon as you got in the vehicle, you told them everything. I mean, it was second nature at this point; they were just as much your parents as they were mine. Since kindergarten, we've been joined at the hip, and you had stayed over more times than at your own house. So as soon as the doors shut, you spilled the truth; the past weeks tumbled from your lips until you had run dry and could only cry.

They comforted you on the way home and stayed by you as you fell asleep in my old room, preserved as if nothing had changed. As if I were still here, and you could wake up the next morning and I'd be there again. It's been the only time you've been able to cry about me since I left.

***

Yet, life plods forward, deaf to your cries for reprieve.

Tim quit smoking, but you can still smell the smoke, even now. Everything is touched by the acrid scent of burnt wood and decomposing plants; sickeningly sweet. Being near Tim strengthens the smell until it's suffocating. At night, it even shows in your dreams. Sometimes, you think it emanates from Tim's lighter, which he still carries everywhere but refuses to use. If he can smell it, he doesn't mention it.

Martin used to scoff at your superstitious habits, engrained into you like a religion. Now, he practices alongside you, a devout believer. Along his windowsill are herbs, which burn your nose and clog it. He's begun to craft wards with them, and he packages them with iron filings and silver chips. If he talks to you, it's only about new ways to fend the *Things* off.

Still, it's better than the empty words from Tim and the wall of silence between you and Sasha.

Sasha never wanted to be involved. She thought you were lying about me, but then again, she never believed in the supernatural, and nothing she saw would change that. It didn't matter that I had all but become a different person overnight; the *Fey* weren't real, and I was still there. Even though you knew me better than she could have, in her mind, there was no way I was gone. She's gotten accepted into a new school, and you hope she can move on after she transfers.

You have other matters to worry about, though. Concerns stronger than Sasha's silence, and Tim's denial, and Martin's diligence. *Its* final words haunt you.

"May you become as I am."

You dread this curse, and yet you know it's already begun. Soon, iron will burn, and Martin's wards will keep you out too. Eventually, you will be gone, and all that will remain will be an uncanny duplicate. You will become the eerie facsimile that haunts you, with a smile too wide and vacant eyes.

***

You have fallen into a routine. The librarians recognize you on sight and will let you stay after close as you pour over every book you can find on folklore. They think you're writing a dissertation, and you haven't done anything to suggest otherwise.

You have piles of books around the apartment, accompanied by scribbled notes. It fills all the gaps I left. My room stays empty; renting it out is still too painful to consider. The apartment is suffocating, but you don't have many alternatives. Still, the loneliness is hard to shake, even as your fate looms above you like a guillotine.

When you get too frustrated at your lack of progress, you'll seek *Them* out to try and pry answers from them, only to leave more confused than you were before. *They* speak in circles and hypotheticals,

103

and *their* words are hypnotic and poetic. *Their* hungry eyes watch you with interest; *They* want to see if you'll escape *their* web before you're consumed by the curse you struggle under.

Everyone knows that you struggle in vain.

You know how this will end. Another fire, another shed. You will be sealed in, with a barrier of salt and binds of silver. Tim's lighter will ignite the dry grass, and you will feel the fire cleanse you. Martin and Tim will watch you from the doorframe, a silent vigil to your death. They will lie, just as you did. They will be the only ones who know what happened to you, just as you three hold the answer to my fate.

The Incineration Plant

by Milo O'Connor

Many people know what it's like to despise their workplace, but I have been traumatized within these walls. This place masquerades itself as an incineration plant, but I've known its true nature for a long time. This job takes its toll on the conscience. It's tough for any person to make it out alive, but I have lost too much at the hands of this company to allow them to take my sanity. Besides, I've got my mission and my team. I won't rest until I take this place down. That is what keeps me going.

I clock in and prepare myself for another day in hell. The cold concrete walls greet me as I enter and all I can hear is the senseless noise. It's so loud I can't make out anything. I walk to my locker and retrieve my earplugs. I always take the cheapest ones they have. They muffle the sound enough to think while allowing me to stay alert. Alertness is the only way I've stayed alive. I grab my nose plugs for good measure. I don't want to know what I'm disposing of today.

Most days, this job is overstimulating. The loud noises and smells of the waste overwhelm me without my plugs. It's so hot in here. Sometimes it feels like I'm the one being burned alive. This job is both my punishment and my penance. I need to do this for my son and other people like him.

I begin stoking the flames of the incinerator. It's a massive metal giant, looming over the floor like an industrial angel of destruction. Once it gets going, it can dispose of large amounts of waste and other undesirables. There's a new hire in training, which means I have an important job to do. I need to warn the poor sucker before it's too late. I drop the letter in his locker when no one is looking.

New Kid,

I've seen you around. You seem like a nice enough kid, too nice to be working at a place like this. You've only been here a couple of days, but that's long enough to know something is off about this place. This is not an authorized plant we are dealing with. Our employers are not city workers, and they are dangerous. Most days will be normal, but you will be asked to dispose of questionable things, like human remains. This is revolting but know that you share these horrors with the rest of us.

You must do your job well, or you will end up in that incinerator. I'm not saying this to scare you, but you must know what's coming. Stay Alert, Stay Alive. There are people you can trust here working to take this company down. People like me. I don't expect you to take my word for it, so I'll level with you. I lost my son. He started working here and suddenly went missing. I knew something was wrong. I changed my name and started working here. My team is working to bring them to justice. Your only job is to survive. Do your job. Fly under the radar of management as much as possible. Escaping their notice is the best way you can stay safe. Don't ask too many questions. Be a competent worker.

I imagine right now you would like to quit. I wish I could tell you to get far away from here, but they won't let you. Follow my instructions and you will make it out alive. I promise.

Be Careful.

A Co-Worker

***

I wish I could do more for the new hires. Hopefully he heeds my warning.

After that, I return to the demands of my job. It's muscle memory at this point. I heave bags of waste into the incinerator and think of my team. This job would drive me to madness without them. It's me and four co-workers who have lost as much as I have. We are putting everything we have into taking this company down. I couldn't do it alone. One of my allies is a lawyer who lost his kid the same way I did. We are gathering enough intel to bring them down. I have faith that we will, someday.

As I'm throwing waste into the huge metal incinerator, I lift an unmistakably heavy bag. My heart sinks. This is the hardest part. Knowing what I'm disposing of and doing it anyway because that's the price of working here.

"Forgive me," I whisper, and toss the human remains in the incinerator.

I will do whatever it takes to bring them down. I will dispose of whatever they tell me to. This is to honour my son and ensure they don't hurt anyone else. I go on autopilot as I continue disposing of waste. This continues for hours until I feel a tap on my shoulder.

"Hi, John. Mind if we have a quick chat?" asks Ben, my supervisor.

I nod and follow him. We walk into his office, where several security guards are lying in wait. This office is nicer than anything else in the building. It has a fancy desk with a leather chair. The thugs currently trying to intimidate me do take away from the elegance of the office.

"We hear you've been warning your co-workers," says Ben.

I nod as the security guards loom over me, waiting for the boss's orders.

"We can't have that," says Ben. "The only way out of here is in a body bag. You will dispose of those bodies and just be grateful you're not one of them."

Ben nods and the guard closes in. One of them punches me in the gut repeatedly, where the bruising won't show. The other one twists my arm behind my back, making it clear he could break it if I don't fall in line.

"There is no escape. In here, we are the law. Stop talking to your co-workers or we will take you out," Ben says.

The guards continue roughing me up, punching and kicking me where it won't be obvious. They know better than to leave visible injuries for my first known infraction.

"Have we made ourselves clear?" Ben asks.

I nod. Then I get back to my work. I don't say another word until lunch when it's safe to talk to my team.

"Did you get all that?" I ask, knowing our lawyer friend insisted on everyone wearing body cams.

"Oh yeah, we finally have everything we need to take them down."

I smile. Our team finally did it. They may have roughed me up, but they won't be hurting people much longer. This place is going down.

The Smell of Gasoline

by Abigail Wallingford

It was the second time the shed had caught fire, and this time I was happy to watch it burn. I wasn't worried, at least on the outside. I had thought long and hard about this and planned to the point where I was second-guessing everything. Now, there was nothing to do but move ahead with the rest of my plan. I was all in. I took a deep breath and got up slowly, stretching as I made my way to the kitchen to grab myself a beer. In the pitch dark, I watched the flames from the kitchen window. I took a sip and walked out to the backyard porch, sat down, raised the bottle in toast, and quietly breathed, "Here's to you, sweetheart."

***

That morning, I woke up to the sound of my alarm. As always, I walked down the stairs and avoided the loud, creaking steps. My husband was still asleep, and I'd been in no rush to wake him. I used to be happy to greet the day and him every morning, fueled by the enthusiasm of newlywed bliss. We had plans to turn the farm into a boutique wedding venue, and I was finally going to own my own business doing what I loved. Apparently, I missed the fine print on our marriage certificate. The veil was quickly whipped away, and I discovered what a liar he was and what a blind fool I had been. Two years later, his boss laid him off, and he became increasingly violent. Almost six months after he carried me over the threshold, it started. Any mistake I'd make would invariably be one I'd regret. At first, the assault was only verbal, but it quickly became physical. I was left battered and bruised daily.

I made breakfast and finished my morning chores in a daze. He soon woke and came downstairs, grumbling about something I'd done. My heart immediately began to race. As he sat and ate, he started up again, berating me for all the perceived imperfections he felt I had made throughout the morning. I stood and nodded. Yup. Sure. Whatever.

I was so tired and done. I didn't want any more pain. I was tired of the sympathetic glances from people in town, tired of always chickening out and not pressing charges. He'd literally hammered and moulded his own fate through me, and I was going to deliver. I went to clean up the breakfast dishes to get out of his line of fire, and not long after, he slammed his way out the door for the day.

I knew that night, like every other, he'd be drinking in the city until late. He would come home in a drunken rage, most likely from a gambling loss. I was lying awake; my heart was beating out of my chest, and I felt the walls shake as he slammed the door upon his return. I heard him grab a beer from the fridge and exit the house through the back door. I knew that something could backfire, that I might be suspected, but I was ready. I had planned and hoped I'd rehearsed enough. It would look exactly as it did the first time when it really was an accident. My husband used the shed for his projects; he was a welder, so he kept all his tools and supplies in there. One of these supplies was gasoline; the shed always reeked of it. The first fire started quickly when he was welding, and a spark landed on a gasoline-soaked rag he used for cleaning. He tried to simply run out of the building only to discover the door was locked. Then he grabbed the extinguisher and was able to contain it to an isolated section of the shed. Just my luck. I had called the fire department in a panic. He got a fine. I got a black eye. However, he hadn't learned any lessons and still stored everything in the same place.

The night of the second fire, while he was out drinking, I opened a barrel of gasoline and doused the shed. All I had to do was wait for him to go in to work on something and let his welding sparks fly. I got out of bed, looking out the window to see that he was crossing the yard to the shed. I moved swiftly down the stairs in my nightgown and stepped into my boots to race to the shed door. I peered in the window to watch him prepare his mask and tools. He didn't see the puddles on the floor or the extra rags I'd placed on the shelves. I quickly flipped the bolt on the outside lock and looked in once more. Sparks flew, and I tore away from the building. I heard the fire start, heard his curses that quickly turned into screams, and then nothing but the popping of burning wood.

I waited until I knew my job was done to set my beer down, then dialed 911. I frantically screamed at the operator for the fire department and ambulance to come. I knew it would take them a while because we lived so far out. I played the part of the distraught wife and explained that this had happened before. I told them of the many times I'd asked him to fix that damn lock. I went through the motions of grief and guilt, though I really didn't regret a thing, and I made it through this safely and never have to worry again.

There was, of course, questioning, and I remained calm and collected on the outside while panicking on the inside. It went on for days. They knew what kind of man he was; they'd seen my bruises and tried to convince me to press charges. They asked the same things over and over again, changing how they would ask them to try and make me falter. I recited my story again and again. I was asleep; he must have come home late and gone to the shed to work; the broken lock must've closed him in. I woke up to the smoke and called the fire department immediately. I was freaking out on the inside, convinced I was going to be charged. They would find something I had missed or that didn't make sense.

Turns out, it doesn't matter if you put on an Oscar-worthy performance for the police and get away with murder. His friends and family will never believe you. I started receiving death threats, and all four of my tires were slashed twice. I woke up in the middle of the night to glass smashing in my living room after someone had thrown a half-full can of gas through the window. One night after work, while I was driving home, a truck came up behind me quickly and rode my bumper, forcing me to speed up. Too scared to pull over, I raced ahead in my little car and barely made it into my driveway before the truck took out my mailbox. It turned around and sat in my driveway for hours. Calls to the police amounted to nothing. The officer who responded was a friend of my husband, and he informed me there was nothing he could do since no one had done anything wrong. It was then that I decided I had to leave, so

I sold the house to a land developer to do whatever he wanted with it. I worked quickly with a realtor and bought a little condo on the beach in Coronado, California, for a fresh start.

I quickly moved the night after the sale and worked on packing whatever would fit in my old truck. I should have done this in the first place—up and left. My plan may have worked perfectly, but in a small town, I was always going to pay for what even the law said I didn't do. So I taped up the last box and placed it in the passenger back seat, hopped into the driver's seat, and stared at my house of broken dreams. I put the truck in reverse just as the wind picked up, smiling as I inhaled because, for a moment, I swear in that moment, I could smell gasoline.

The Ghost Fire

by Kaela Pacheco

It was the second time the shed had caught fire. It seemed to occur so naturally. It was as if the dry summer air mixed with a cool yet warm breeze caused the spark. It was like flint against steel. The fire had spooked the town. The first fire was thought to be caused by some natural phenomenon, but after the second fire, they thought otherwise. Strange, phenomenal events often occurred in the small town of Astracane, so the second fire wasn't all that weird.

The shed was in the middle of the woods in the eastern part of town. Whenever you got close to the shed, you'd feel like you were being watched. If you were alone, you'd get a chill down your spine, and the hairs on the back of your neck would stand up. If you were with friends, all you got was an uncomfortable and ominous feeling.

Since I didn't have television, I often bought the newspaper down the street with my parents' money. When I saw the news about the second fire, I got chills down my spine. I went down to the shed last night and investigated the reason for the first fire on my own. I told no one about it. I couldn't, or they'd think I started the fire.

I took a copy of the newspaper from the dinner table and went up to my room. With the newspaper tucked underneath my armpit, I opened the closet door. I flipped on the light switch, and my closet came to life. I walked toward the back and grabbed a pair of scissors. I held the newspaper in my hand. I cut the news article out about the shed fire and pinned it to my bulletin board. I threw out the rest of the newspaper and shut my closet door once I turned the light off. I sat on my bed and grabbed my phone. I turned it on and looked at my contacts, even though I only had four of them. My mom, my dad, my sister, and my best friend. I decided to turn my phone off before I placed it on my side table. I didn't need to call or text anyone.

I looked out my window. I lived out east, so you could see the forest clearly from my place. It unsettled me to look at the forest strangely enough, but it was normal that I felt that kind of feeling. I looked away from my window and lay down. I shut my eyes, and I drifted off to sleep.

***

What...? Where am I...? I rubbed my eyes sheepishly and looked at my surroundings. I was in the forest. Trees surrounded me and towered over me. I turned around, and my eyes widened. There it was. The shed. A chill ran down my spine, and the hairs on the back of my neck stood on end.

Before I could take another step towards the shed, a shrill scream ripped through the air. A figure stood in front of the shed. It was a woman. Her dress was white, brittle, and charred. Her flesh was shriveling. Bone was exposed where the thin layers of flesh were. They almost looked like burns. She turned and looked at me. Her eyes were sunken and hollow, just like her cheeks.

"Did you die here?" I asked cautiously. So many questions had popped up in my head. *What happened to her? How did this woman become like this?* She suddenly burst into flames and lunged at me. I screamed and fell onto my back as she grabbed onto me. I tried to push her off, but my arms felt so heavy. I felt a searing pain as the woman grabbed my wrists. It felt as if they were on fire. I screamed louder. *How do I get her off me?* I clenched my eyes shut and hoped this was a nightmare. "Ethan!" *That voice!* "Wake up Ethan! Fuck! Wake the hell up!" *My wrists... they hurt so damn much.* "Ethan!" That voice called me again. "Come on Ethan! You have to wake up! I need you to wake up!" My eyes snapped open, and I bolted upright as I gasped for air. "Ethan, are you alright?" I looked beside me to my left to see my mom looking at me with a worried expression. "I think so," I replied, staring down at my wrists instinctively. My mom's eyes widened, and she gently grabbed my wrists to examine them. I slowly sat up so she could look at my them better. They felt searing hot, but I had no reaction to how much it hurt. They were bruised and tender to the touch. Mom got up, grabbed the first-aid kit from the bathroom, and came back into the room. She then sat beside me, opened the first-aid kit, grabbed the cooling gel, opened the package, and applied the gel to my wrists. The cold sensation on my wrists felt nice. I could finally relax. My mom put the first-aid kit away before she came to sit beside me. "Did you go toward the shed?" Mom asked. "I did," I replied shamefully. I felt obliged to tell her the truth. I couldn't lie to her. She's my mom. She looked at me with a sorrowful look. Why? I didn't understand. "I missed you so much," Mom said softly. "I don't know what you mean," I replied as I looked her in the eyes. "You've been here the entire time, haven't you?" "It's been so long since I've seen you like this." Her tone was soft and fragile. It was like she could break if I stayed here any longer. I didn't understand. I felt a hand on my shoulder, and I turned around to see the woman from before. She looked like the girl I saw in my dream, but she didn't have those burns or marks on her. "Who are you?" I asked her.

"I'm your sister," the girl replied softly.

"I don't understand," I muttered and stumbled back. "What's going on?" A smile was plastered on her face. I turned around to see Mom was gone. Where did she go? The floor shook, and the house was crumbling down. *What's going on?*

"You don't remember, do you?" she asked and looked perplexed. My head felt like it was spinning. I didn't understand what was going on. What was I supposed to remember? I looked at my sister with a confused expression. "What do you mean?" I questioned. "Father burned us during the witch trials," she explained. "I looked scary to you because you couldn't accept the fact you were dead." I blinked a few times while I looked at her. *Was she the woman in that dream? I was... dead? How? That's impossible...*

I don't remember dying. Perhaps it was just a long time? Was it that long ago? "Do you remember?" she asked. "No," I replied.

"It's better you don't remember," my alleged sister told me. "We shall go back to the shed." I nodded, and she grabbed my hand. I followed her out of the house towards the forest. I felt like I had to follow her. I trusted her, but I didn't know why. I just did. A missing piece of memory. It all flooded back to me. We walked up toward the shed and right up to the door. My sister opened it up. A bright light filled my vision, and I squinted. With one look toward her, I smiled. She smiled back. We both then walked toward the bright light, hand in hand. If you're wondering about the fire, I have one thing to tell you. You could probably still find it back there if you looked hard enough.

Cowboys and Angels

by Angie Mosher

A Cowboy walked into a bar.

He was late. He was always late. Being on time was embarrassing, being early—unthinkable. He didn't like Manhattan. His contempt made him even later than usual. Tourists stopped him everywhere, took in his spurs and boots, his belt, his cow-hide jacket and asked, *Can we take a picture with you?* He never did. He pulled his hat down over his forehead and said, n*o can do. I ain't from here neither.* Sometimes they laughed. Other times they'd get angry. He would just walk away.

It was raining miserably. Water dripped from the brim of his hat, soaked the fringe of his coat. He took it off, gave it a shake, and put it back on. The Angel was already there, in the corner booth, perched on the velvet cushion, drinking a gin and tonic. She was aglow, as usual; the dim lighting of the bar was nothing compared to her. The Cowboy saw her at once. He went over to the bartender and ordered a bourbon, neat. When he turned to join Angel in her booth, she was there, on the stool beside him. He offered her a smile, tipping his hat to her in greeting.

"Do you remember when we met?" the Angel asked in her melodic voice.

"Couldn't forget that, darlin'."

He'd been bleeding out in a dirt patch of a ditch, in the dead nowhere of Wyoming. That had been a year ago.

"This is a better place, then," the Angel said.

It sounded like a question, so he answered it like one.

"Maybe."

She nodded at that and took a sip of her drink. The bartender returned and placed the bourbon in front of him. He picked it up and took a small sip.

He looked better in some ways and worse in others, she thought. His clothes were cleaner, his boots were shinier, but his shoulders sagged. His pistol was missing. The scar on his face divided him in two, a jagged line cutting from his left eyebrow, marring the eyelid, clouding the eye, sinking down through the bridge of his nose to settle just above the right corner of his lip. She had sewn the wound shut herself. He was still so beautiful. He was still hers.

"Been busy lately?" he asked, his voice gruff, deeper than it was when they first met.

She had been. She was busy in Manhattan. Hell's Kitchen especially. Not so many angels out there. That's why she'd left L.A. She stopped in Wyoming, not really sure where she was going. She stopped in small towns and found lost souls, hoping she'd find a place worth staying. Meeting people at the end of their lives was wearing on her. She had been losing her light for a long time. Then she found her Cowboy.

She was tired of helping souls to Heaven and he was tired of the Wild West. They fell in love, and fled together to the big city. He became a butcher in Brooklyn, and she stood on street corners and rooftops, saving souls. They shared a small apartment in the bottom of a brownstone. They didn't see each other as much as they wanted to. He understood. She was important. Sometimes, he'd stand on street corners with her and play guitar. He worried about her in the city, by herself. Not everyone cared about angels. He knew she'd been hurt before. Sometimes a dark mood would take her, and there was nothing that he could do. He knew then she was remembering past lives and past pain, things that were beyond him. Sometimes she wouldn't come home for days. He'd slice into raw flesh all day, only to come home to nobody, and wait for her all night. Sometimes, he'd pray and imagined she could hear him, wherever she was.

So they met in the same bar every Sunday. It was almost a date, a way to see each other outside of crawling into bed, or a quick kiss on the cheek before they left to go where they needed to be. He'd make his way over from Brooklyn and she would be there, glowing, waiting, her head bowed over a drink as if deep in prayer.

"What have you been doing?" she asked. He took another sip of his bourbon.

"Workin'. Walkin'. Not much else to do."

"In a city like this?"

He nodded. She understood. He was a man of the land. Not concrete. Not trains and subways. Not for the first time, she felt guilty for bringing him there.

"You hate it here."

He brought the glass of bourbon to his mouth and poured it back, slamming the glass down on the bar, harder than he'd meant to, so hard that the bottom of the glass splintered out with cracks. She didn't flinch. She was used to his darker moods, too.

"You want to leave." She said it simply. She'd known for a while. She'd been pressed down into the shape of a woman, for more than a few decades. Longer than he'd been alive, longer than she had cared to be. She'd known every kind of heartbreak. This one felt new.

"You want to leave the city. You want to leave me."

He did not look at her. He stared into the cracks of his glass, like he could will the splintering into smoothness. She had always looked at him like he wasn't a broken thing—not half a man, not a weak lover, like he was something whole. It was a sacred thing, but he could not help shattering under her holy gaze.

For a while, neither of them spoke. She finished her drink, he ordered another. He glowered; she glowed. After finishing his second bourbon, he found his voice.

"Why didn't you leave me there? To die?"

Whatever she had been expecting him to say, it wasn't that. He looked at her then, really looked at her. He sounded angry, resigned. He suddenly felt his age. It was hard to feel old in her spectral company, but he felt very old then. It occurred to him, when he took in the sad look upon her face, that she must have felt the same way.

"Why did you come with me? To this city?" Her voice rang out clear like a bell.

"It ain't fair to answer a question with another question."

"What is fair?"

He didn't know. That day in the ditch, he thought that he'd known. He'd made his peace with dying, that had seemed fair. Then, there she was.

"I didn't want to be alone anymore," he said, finally. She stared up at him, waiting. He didn't know what else to say. That was the simple truth of it. He'd decided that he'd met his fate and she had appeared and tore him away from it. When he first saw her, he understood what all the songs were about, why he'd said every prayer as a boy, bent on that wooden pew in the church his Ma had dragged him to. He squinted through the blood with his one good eye and saw her glistening face. She'd given him a reason to live. He loved her for it, but now, he thought maybe he hated her for it.

"Tell me. Why couldn't you just let me die?"

She'd seen many men die. Greater men than him. She watched their eyes roll into the back of their heads, seen the snap of bones and heard the final beats of their hearts. She brought them from this world to the next. Not once had she intervened. Not once did she feel like she had to. But even God's love left a lot to be desired. She wanted someone to love her because they chose to.

"I didn't want to be alone anymore, either."

"Well, shit."

He wanted her to say that it was God's Plan—that he hadn't been meant to die and was destined for greater things. That was the only reason an angel would tear up the dirt road in a Silverado and stitch him back together in the back seat. No more ranching, no more fighting, no more shooting. God's damn plan.

She sighed and waved the bartender down for another gin and tonic. He ordered another bourbon. She usually only had one drink. She never used to drink at all. She usually left men to their own devices. She usually didn't take lovers. She had fallen in love with him. He had asked her once, when they were laying in bed, if she had done that often. She'd answered honestly, that she hadn't, and couldn't puzzle out if he was relieved or not. Her Cowboy was only a man. She wouldn't ask him to be more.

"Remember when you taught me the two-step?"

He laughed. To his surprise, she was a terrible dancer. They were hiding out in a barn, still in Wyoming. Dolly Parton sang through the truck radio and he tried teaching her how to two-step. She had no rhythm, no sense of her feet or how to move them. He thought she could do anything, but watching her trip over herself made her seem just as human as he was. He teased her, *what, they don't teach you to dance in heaven?* She laughed, radiating light and said, *not like this.* It was the first time he could remember being so happy, watching an angel fall over her own feet. When she gave up, they held each other and just swayed to whatever the radio played.

"That was the best night of my life," he said, smiling at the memory. She smiled at him, and felt a wistful tug at her heart. Her eyes watered, but no tears fell.

"Mine, too."

She never learned to use her feet like that, didn't think she'd ever need to. Her Cowboy taught her a lot of new things that she didn't think she'd ever do. Sometimes, he'd shock her with just how gentle he could be; the way he had held her that night, so tenderly with calloused hands. Her calm demeanour broke ever-so slightly.

"Where will you go?" she asked. He startled at that, breaking out of the reverie.

"Who said I'm goin' anywhere?"

"You don't have to say it. I've been a lot of things. I've never been a fool." He sobered at that. He didn't have the will to fight anymore, or to lie. If anything had died in the ditch, it was that.

"Back to Wyoming," he said. She knew that, just needed him to say it. Needed to hear it. She might have begged him to stay, but they both had their pride. Just another thing she had learned from him.

"You'll die there." It wasn't an ill-wish, she wasn't a lover scorned. He didn't seem shocked or scared by her statement, he only took another sip of his drink. It was expensive stuff, not the kind he was used to. Only she would pick a place like this to say goodbye. His eyes burned with tears, and for once, he didn't fight them.

"Let me ask you one more thing. When I die, I'll have loved you forever. Can you say the same?"

The Angel hung her head. Oh, her foolish cowboy. He didn't know what forever was. That was how long it had been until she'd found him. That's how long it would be without him. She watched as he stood and paid his tab. He turned to her, sitting on the stool, shining in her white light, weeping softly. She closed her eyes as he laid a gentle kiss on her golden head.

She let herself look at him one last time and thought of that night they danced together. He had loved her, and that was enough.

"I'll always love you, Cowboy."

He tipped his hat to her again and walked out the door.

Contributors

AILSA ALLAN was born and raised in Ancaster, Ontario. Growing up, she immersed herself in fictional worlds to hide from reality. Now, Ailsa works towards a Professional Writing degree at Algonquin College, where she can spend her time creating her own worlds professionally. When she's not writing, you can find her cuddled up on the couch with her dogs or out in a field riding her horse. You can check out more of Ailsa's writing on Instagram @ailsa.is.writing.

COMET C. was born and raised in Ottawa, Ontario. Ever since they were little, they loved writing stories, especially comics. Nowadays, they're making it their goal to make more LGBTQ+ books and characters in media because that's what their younger self would've loved.

ALEX CUVELIER is a writer from Nova Scotia currently enrolled in the Professional Writing program at Algonquin College. He fell in love with poetry in school and published his first poem in *Jump Over the Moon* at the age of 11. "Letters From Home" is his first piece published in the many years since then, but his love of writing and storytelling has never changed.

REY DEL R. is a passionate writer who loves to create fantasy. He is currently studying at Algonquin College. His interests are watching anime, reading manga, and finding ways to improve for the better.

GREGORY DICKEY is an author from Ottawa who writes silly stories about space, birds, and the beauty of all things.

JACK DINGWALL grew up in Lakeside, Ontario, a town so small it didn't even have a gas station. A horror lover, Jack has many morbid fascinations. When he was 13, he wrote his first horror short about a family being eaten alive by a demon. He currently attends Algonquin College and resides in Ottawa despite not being able to tolerate cold weather.

ZOE FARMER was born and raised in a small town called Brockville in the beautiful province of Ontario. Zoe has always been fascinated with scary characters and played with dolls, which she called "The Chucky Dolls." This led to her passion for writing horrific novels. When she's not writing her horror stories, you can find her watching scary movies or walking around the remarkable city of Ottawa at night.

DALAINEY GERVAIS is a writer and artist from Toronto, Ontario. She holds a BA in Linguistics from the University of Toronto and is a student at Algonquin College's Professional Writing program. Currently working in the non-profit sphere, she hopes to develop a career in environmental policy writing. In her free time, Dal enjoys knitting, baking, and watching the latest crime documentary on Netflix.

CHRIS HODGINS was born in Nova Scotia but currently lives in Ontario, and still misses the smell of the sea. He enjoys video games and D&D and loves his wife and furry kids more than anything else. "A Date with Destiny" is his first short story and combines his love of fantasy with his sarcastic sense of humour.

H. ISSAQ is a Somali-Canadian writer with a head full of nonsense. She enjoys exploring different genres and forms of writing and pushing herself to learn new things. She has recently begun the practice of taking herself less seriously and incorporating more of her own humor and personality into her work. Hence... this.

JOEL is an aspiring writer and a horror buff. They have seen horror movies numbering in the hundreds (gore squick be damned), and hope to be a horror writer themself one day. This little spit of writing is far from their first endeavour into horror ... though it is the first one to get officially published.

GARRETT JOHNSON is an aspiring fantasy writer currently studying at Algonquin College and Carleton University. When he's not busy devising a million different plots he'll never get around to actualizing, he likes to work out with friends, play video games, watch anime, sing karaoke, and make funny voice impressions of fictional characters (to varying degrees of success).

C.KANEWAY started their adult life with a brief career in microelectronic engineering, and then tried to trade it for a career in the video game industry before remembering their oldest love. Since their earliest childhood, C.Kaneway has had a runaway imagination pushing them towards fantasy, science-fiction, and world-building. *Pup* isn't their typical style of short-story, but it still puts their best foot forward.

EIRINI KATSIKA is a second-year student at Algonquin College pursuing a degree in Professional Writing. She is an aspiring writer and an avid reader. She always found solace in fictional worlds and wrote her first book when she was 15. When not immersed in the world of writing, Eirini Katsika can be found curating literary wonders on her Bookstagram account. She currently lives in Ottawa, Canada with her husband and their three-legged dog.

WILLIAM KEIZER is an Ottawa-based writer interested in horror fiction. He is currently studying Professional Writing at Algonquin College. "Invited In" is his first published work.

SARAH LAHAISE is an author of many interests and inspirations. Thanks to a love of storytelling, she has developed a unique writing style and a love of writing. Even when she's hyper-fixating on something, snuggling her cat, or crafting, she's writing a story.

AMY LAWFORD is a third-year Professional Writing student at Algonquin College. She was born and raised in Ottawa, Ontario. Professional Writing has been a passion for many years. Keep an eye out for her next book!

As an Ottawa author, OWEN MCDONALD takes pride in his Canadian roots while writing fiction inspired by the chronic loneliness he struggled with as a teen. He also battles an alliteration addiction. But in those spare moments when he's not lining up consonants, he also likes to sit in the sun—sipping coffee while reading some Sanderson. "What You Missed" is Owen's first published piece of fiction.

ANGIE MOSHER is a writer living in Ottawa, Ontario. She's originally from Halifax, Nova Scotia, and misses the ocean dearly. She has a Bachelor of Arts in Creative Writing from the University of British Columbia and is currently studying Professional Writing at Algonquin College. She's had her poetry published in the journal *That's What We Said*, *The Phoenix News* and UBC's *Papershell Anthology*. "Cowboys and Angels" is her first published short story. When she's not writing, she's probably at home with her cats, playing video games, or planning her next tattoo.

As a lifelong connoisseur of film and literature, GARETH MYERS has always held a deep passion for the craft of storytelling. Being the very stereotype of a basement dwelling nerd, he is well versed in the areas of sci-fi, fantasy, anime, videogames, and more. He takes no shame in drawing influence from these sources, though takes the most joy in finding new ways of slamming these influences together in the most bizarrely effective combinations.

REBECCA NICHOLSON is an Algonquin College student in the Professional Writing program. She also graduated with a Bachelor of Psychology from Carleton University. Rebecca has a passion for feminism and political justice. She spends her free time writing and playing video games.

MILO O'CONNOR is a Professional Writing student who loves the art of storytelling. This is their second published work after contributing to the "Beyond the Barriers" charity zine. Keep a look out for their upcoming children's book, "Ghost Outfits Are Forever." When they aren't writing, they can be found playing Dungeons & Dragons and spending time with friends.

KAELA PACHECO, who resides in Canada, has been writing since she was eight years old and enjoys her craft. She enjoys a good book and photography as well. She also likes drawing and long car drives. She loves travelling too. Her favourite place to write is outside or in silence in her room.

EMILY-ANN PETAWABANO is a Professional Writing student at Algonquin College in Ottawa. She loves being with her family, especially all three of her brothers. She spends her time at home cooking and playing video games online with her friends.

VALERIE ROBERT is a young inspiring author who grew up in Ottawa, Ontario, Canada. When she's not spending her time reading and writing, she's with her family and learning new skills. Her first short story, "Key to A Dead Man's Grave," will leave you with questions and chills.

NICHOLAS SAUMUR is an aspiring author who enjoys writing all kinds of stories, although he is usually drawn to horror. The goal of his stories is to entertain and try out new ideas. If you end up learning something or reflecting on one of his stories, it's just a bonus.

EDWIN SMITH has been in Ottawa since birth. Over the years, he's developed a love for fiction writing; and, as of 2023, is in his second-year as a professional writing student. Most of his stories follow the style of literary works; however, they're always paired with fantastical elements. He also spends some time composing music and painting, though these have always been secondary to his writing.

R. SOLITAIRO grew up in a small town in Ontario. Growing up they loved all things creepy and unknown. They love pulling from their life experiences and their latest interest.

ABIGAIL WALLINGFORD is a writer living in Ottawa, Ontario. She is currently in her second year studying Professional Writing at Algonquin College. She is an avid reader and, of course, has quite the TBR. She plans to travel after graduation and use her experiences in her next series of works. Her family actively and lovingly supports her, and she finds snuggling with one of the four dogs in the house as a good brain break when trying to find direction.

PAIGE WELBURN is a second-year student in the Professional Writing Program at Algonquin College. She graduated high school in 2021 with a Red Seal Diploma. She enjoys creative writing, and mostly writes fantasy stories. Paige spends her spare time playing Sledge hockey, playing video games, and going camping in the summer.

CHASE WONNACOTT is a Professional Writing student at Algonquin College. He is from Southern Ontario, and if you asked him what town, he would give you a different answer every time. Upon seeing Chase in the wild, know there will always be music playing. Although sometimes that music is just in his mind, that won't stop him from dancing to it—especially if he finds the world too quiet.